AZETTE FROM JERSEY

When Azette flew from Jersey to the West Country, to find her favourite cousin Dennis, she also made new friends: Jane, now her flat-mate, and Mandy, who refuses to name her baby's father and needs help. At Jane's family home Azette is introduced to Andrew, a handsome — if moody — farmer . . . She is reunited with her cousin Dennis, but suddenly their relationship changes, and their plans to return to Jersey together crumble. Now Azette has a difficult decision to make . . .

IRENE CASTLE

AZETTE FROM JERSEY

Complete and Unabridged

LINFORD
Leicester

First published in Great Britain in 1974 by
Robert Hale Ltd
London

First Linford Edition
published 2008
by arrangement with
Robert Hale Ltd
London

British Library CIP Data

Castle, Irene
    Azette from Jersey.—Large print ed.—
Linford romance library
1. Love stories
2. Large type books
I. Title
823.9'14 [F]

ISBN 978–1–84782–295–6

Published by
F. A. Thorpe (Publishing)
Anstey, Leicestershire

Set by Words & Graphics Ltd.
Anstey, Leicestershire
Printed and bound in Great Britain by
T. J. International Ltd., Padstow, Cornwall

This book is printed on acid-free paper

For my daughter Ruth

1

The sun rose behind the grey Dorset
cliffs, and diffused the sky with gold. A
rocket was sent off from Tollbury
Lifeboat Station; gulls shrieked, Azette
stirred in her strange bed and tried to
leave her disturbing dream. She was
back in Jersey racing across the sands
with her cousin Dennis until the
oncoming tide engulfed him. She was
dreaming she had plunged into a
mountainous wave to find him when a
second rocket woke her fully; it caused
the red-haired girl (called Jane) in the
bed at the other side of the room to
throw back her covers.

'I must find out who is in trouble,
Azette; I know everybody who sails
from the harbour.' Jane fumbled amongst
the clothing scattered on her bedside
rug. 'Back soon.' She dragged denim
slacks over her shortee nightdress. 'Make

1

some tea.' She wriggled into a brown pullover.

Azette knelt on her bed to watch Jane run barefoot along the promenade towards the harbour. A steamer moved slowly on the horizon, and the calm sea gently slapped the prow of a fishing trawler which was heading inshore. Azette pressed her fair head against the window pane, soon she saw the lifeboat head westwards. When it was out of sight, she took her blue dressing-gown from her suitcase and went into the sitting-room; she threw open the curtains before turning into the kitchenette to put the kettle on. Jane kept this cubby hole tidier than her bedroom; she had washed last night's coffee cups, and had stood three yellow cups and saucers on a tray beside a brown tea-pot. Azette was wondering who the third cup was for when a gentle voice asked from the doorway:

'Please count me in.'

Azette's alert hazel eyes met the soulful dark ones of a raven-haired girl.

'You don't look too good,' she said in concern.

'I'm not,' the girl replied ruefully. She buttoned her plum quilted dressing-gown up to her neck. 'I'm Mandy. My flat is across the passage; it's useful because Jane and I share most things from her early tea to my television.' She reached for a biscuit tin. 'Good. Digestive. They help settle my morning sickness.' She held out her ringless left hand. 'You'd better know right away that I'm not married.' Mandy's lovely oval face was pale and sad. She shivered. 'It's cold for late March.'

'Come and sit by the fire Mandy.' Azette made the tea, took up the tray, led the way into the sitting-room and switched on a bar of the electric fire. Mandy curled up on the settee and covered her legs with cushions.

'It's nice to have someone to talk to Azette. Jane said you'd flown from Jersey yesterday to search for your cousin. Tell me about him.'

3

Azette reasoned it might take Mandy's mind off her plight (if it was a plight) if she told her about herself and Dennis. 'His name is Dennis Maxted, he's twenty-three, and has black hair and a beard; perhaps you know him?'

'Sorry, but I don't. How did you lose touch with him?'

'He ran away from home two years ago.'

'Why?' Mandy took another biscuit from the tin.

'Dennis's father (who is my father's first cousin) wanted him to accept a place in a University. Dennis refused; it led to awful rows.'

'Was that Dennis's only crime?'

'Yes. It doesn't sound much, but Uncle Adrian is a brilliant doctor who doesn't suffer fools gladly as they say. He took over his practice from his father, and now his eldest son has a share in it. As his daughter is a nurse, Dennis was expected to do something worth while too.'

'Most jobs are worth while aren't

they? Those lifeboat men, and the fishermen — '

'I agree, but Uncle Adrian is full of self importance, and demanded great things from his children. His wife, Aunty Simone, is sweet and sympathetic, but Uncle Adrian wanted more from Dennis than he could give — so he cleared off.'

'But what did Dennis want to do?'

'He used to say he couldn't find his true self whilst living under his father's roof; Uncle Adrian would squash everything Dennis attempted which didn't need a University backing.'

'That was silly. Has Dennis been in Tollbury for two years?'

'No. He has sent post-cards to his mother from London to stop her worrying, and, sometimes, he remembered me. Then a few weeks ago one of my brothers heard, in a round-about way, that Dennis was working in Tollbury.'

'But why has it been left to you to find him?'

'Because when we were kids Dennis and I were like one person. We are the youngest of our family circle. Dennis arrived like a thunder-bolt and caused quite a stir.'

'Why?'

'Because he was stormy and difficult.'

'And you?'

'I was born at the end of that year so was naturally paired off with Dennis at our family gatherings.'

'But you weren't stormy or difficult, Azette. It's easy to tell that.' Mandy studied Azette thoughtfully. She was poised and calm, but somewhere behind the tranquil expression in her eyes, there lurked a restlessness which Mandy thought might be ignited by a spark — a spark perhaps caught from Dennis. 'I bet you've had lots of boys since Dennis left. You're so attractive, you'd look great even wearing an old sack, Azette.'

'Oh thanks. My mother was very attractive, and still is. They say I take after both her and my father in looks, but that I'm usually as calm and controlled as my father is.'

'Unless you're with Dennis I bet. Did your mother mind your going around with him?'

'No. She says Dennis is like Uncle Adrian's brother, Maurice, who was killed in the war. He ran wild with my mother — but that's another story.' Azette re-filled their tea cups.

Mandy said, 'I work out that Dennis is your third cousin.' Her dark eyes widened curiously. 'Are you in love with him?'

'No, no. It wasn't like that. As far back as I can remember I accepted the fact that Dennis was always around to share my thoughts, my troubles and my fun. Then one day he had gone.'

Azette looked reflectively into the glow of the mock coal fire. On her farm she had sat with Dennis beside fires of coal, apple wood and pine cones; on the beach they had lit fires of drift wood and dried vraic. Mandy broke into her thoughts.

7

'How was it you found your way to Jane's flat?'

'My father warned me it would be difficult to find a room the day before Good Friday. How right he was. I lugged my case up and down this little town until it teemed with rain. The 'bus shelter was packed with black leather jackets; the girls swore and threw toffee papers to get rid of me. But when I told a boy I was looking for a room, he hailed this fellow crossing the road because he was an estate agent. This agent said lodgings weren't his line, but he looked so humane with rain dripping down both brims of his deer stalker, and his dark brows drawn together in concern, that I knew he would help.'

'That was Michael,' Mandy smiled. 'He's a sweetie, and would be Jane's boy friend if she didn't play the fool with so many others.'

'Oh. Well, Michael said Jane had a spare bed. I was a bit dubious about going with him until he told me that although he didn't know Dennis, Jane

8

ought to because she knew everybody in Tollbury. So I let Michael take my case and followed him round to the prom'. But Jane didn't know Dennis.'

'Never mind, if he's here you're bound to find him in time.' Mandy removed the cushions from her legs. 'I'm warmer now.'

'When is your baby due Mandy?'

'Late October.'

'Will you be able to look after it alone?'

'I must; but at present I'm still sort of dazed, and haven't made plans. The dressmaker whom I work for is very kind; I've a sewing machine so she'll give me work to do in my flat if I want to keep the baby. Then I've been left money by my mother. My father married again after she died; I left home because I hated the way my step-mother took my mother's place.' Mandy stood up abruptly. 'I must bath. I've taken on a dish-washing job over the weekend.'

'You mustn't do that you fool,'

protested Jane who had overheard Mandy's remark on entering the room. 'Good Friday is a hectic day, and the smell from the fryer will make you sick again. I'd take over for you if the family hadn't summoned me to lunch.' Jane tossed her red hair in annoyance, and her pretty lips drew back from her teeth. 'Whatever possessed you to take on such a job Mandy?'

'I'm saving all I can for the baby.'

'That's its father's job,' Jane snapped. 'If you'd say who he is, I'd tell him so, and a few other things besides,' Jane uttered vehemently. 'I know you're nineteen, but it's time you realised how tough life can be if you're too soft with men.'

Mandy stared down at her plum-coloured mules in silence.

'I've nothing to do today,' Azette stated decisively. 'I'll take on your dish-washing, Mandy.'

Mandy started to protest, but Jane took a realistic attitude. 'You mean that? What work do you usually do Azette?'

'Secretarial. But I help with all sorts of mucky jobs round the farm. You can bank my Easter dish-washing wages for your baby Mandy.'

When Mandy had gone, Azette asked Jane, 'Why was the lifeboat called out?'

'Terry Guard slipped, and cracked his head on the bow of the pebble picker's boat.'

'Who is Terry Guard?'

'He helps Billy Preston pick pebbles. He fell overboard, and Billy had trouble in hauling him back into the boat because he was stunned.'

'Why do the pebble pickers go out so early?'

'Billy must plan his trips to fit in with the tides; it's a money making job.'

* * *

By half past ten the two girls were ready to leave the flat. Azette wore a blouse and skirt under her yellow raincoat, and carried an overall of Mandy's in a brown paper bag; her fair hair was

11

caught back neatly with a large hair slide. Jane had coiled her red hair into a bun at the nape of her neck; she wore a stylish green suit, a new pair of tights and highly polished brown shoes. Her mouth had been set in a pout since her uncle had telephoned her an hour ago. Did she know the 'buses did not run on Good Friday? No? Then she should have troubled to consult her time table he had growled. No matter, as he hated driving his blasted car, and Monica was doing the flowers, he had asked Andrew Gordon to pick her up from the harbour car park at eleven.

'Bet he's there at a quarter to,' Jane muttered as she stepped out on to the promenade with Azette. 'Just to spite me.'

'How many of your family live in Warren House?' Azette asked.

'There's my father's brother, Uncle George, and his sisters, Aunts Monica and May. They're years older than my father, and he's not all that young — square as they come, but I mustn't

12

grumble because when I had the chance of a job as dental receptionist in Tollbury, my parents said I needn't return to Darkest Africa with them if the family would keep an eye on me. It was hell in Africa — no whites of my age within driving distance.' Jane glanced at her watch. 'It will do Andrew good to wait.'

'Who is Andrew?'

'A neighbouring farmer who has lived at Warren House since his farmhouse was burnt down last year. That happened late one night when he was visiting our local glamour widow — she's married some other sap now. Andrew hates himself because he left a huge fire roaring up an old chimney unattended; he's sort of bitter, but he's under thirty and most girls think he's fantastic.'

'But you don't?'

Jane hedged. 'Aunt Monica thinks he'd be a suitable match for me; I intend having a good time before I marry.'

The girls paused to admire the colourful yachts which slid gracefully out of the harbour. Then Michael caught up with them. His jersey was too tight and his brown hair untidy; he carried a brush in one hand, and a can of paint in the other.

'Aren't you selling houses today Michael?' Jane eyed him scathingly, but Azette suspected this expression was merely assumed.

'I'm going to paint my boat.' Michael fell into step with the girls.

'You ought to be sailing, the wind is perfect,' Jane pointed out.

'I've lost my crew — Tom's bank have transferred him to Plymouth.' Michael regarded Jane hopefully from under his dark brows. 'I may have to resort to asking you to crew for me.'

'Asking me is as far as you'll get. Try asking Azette.'

Azette put in hastily, 'I don't know for how long I'll be in Tollbury. It depends on what Dennis is up to — but I have to find him first.'

'I'll ask around for you.' Michael waved his paint brush in farewell before hurrying down some steps.

Azette watched as he crossed to a stretch of dry sand where children chased their dog around up-turned boats. She questioned Jane:

'Don't you like Michael? Or are you playing hard to get?'

'I like him all right, but, as I've just told you, I don't intend marrying yet.' Jane pointed to a mustard coloured Austin standing in the car park. 'That's Andrew's car.'

Jane laughed as Andrew tooted to hurry her, then she deliberately took her time in saying good-bye to Azette. Finally there was an ear-splitting honk and Andrew's hand beckoned from a window. Jane crossed to him with maddening slowness.

Azette turned to the cafe which stood on the foreshore; it was a little early for her to report for work. She looked across the sparkling sea in the direction of the Channel Isles; it seemed impossible that she had left Jersey less than twenty-four hours ago. She was in a new world and had already become involved in the lives of two new friends, Jane and Mandy. She had not thought that Dennis would be so elusive. Why was it that although Jane knew everybody in Tollbury, she did not know him?

Things had worked out differently from what she had anticipated; Tollbury's population was small, she had expected the first resident she spoke to would know Dennis. Now, as she watched the waves advancing, retreating and criss-crossing, other matters tended to crowd him out of her mind — the helpless appeal in Mandy's dark eyes. Jane's friendly smile but childish behaviour, Michael's breezy kindness and Andrew Gordon's beckoning hand.

2

'This can't be happening to me,' Azette told herself two hours later.

She stood at a scullery sink facing a walled in yard. One draining board was piled high with dirty dishes and sticky silver; an enormous plate rack, stacked with cups and saucers, stood on the other draining board. There was a dish-washer, but Mrs Cornish (the café proprietress) had decreed it was not to be used until Whitsun. A waitress entered with a tray laden with plates; she shot fragments of fish and chips into a waste bin.

'You'll have to move quicker than that,' she warned Azette. 'No time to be fussy.' She swirled a handful of side plates in the washing up bowl. 'That's all you need do.'

Azette soaked the fatty plates whilst whisking the tea towel over the contents of the rack; these must be carried through to the café bar which enabled Azette to take stock of the customers. Dennis could be amongst them. He was not, but Michael shared a table with three young men; they gave Azette a cheerful 'thumbs-up' sign. The stout cook way-laid her on her way back through the kitchen.

'I'm gettin' short of dinner plates Girl,' she spluttered through a mouthful of chips.

Azette hurried back to the sink, and soon returned with a heavy pile of dinner plates which she placed in a warming cupboard for the cook. She was glad she had taken over from Mandy — this job could give a pregnant girl a mis'.

' 'Er's some lunch for you Girl.' The cook clumped a plate of hamburgers and chips on the lid of the waste bin.

'Where shall I sit?' Azette asked.

'Sit!' exploded the woman. 'No time for that in rush 'ours is there — I 'ave my grub whilst I fry.' She waddled back to her kitchen.

Azette judged by the way her greasy white apron bulged that she ate continuously whilst cooking. At three o'clock there was a lull, Azette perched on a cupboard from where she could see a family, dressed in windcheaters and slacks, walking by the water's edge. Doubtless her family and Dennis's would be sharing their traditional Good Friday picnic on a favourite beach. She had always paired off with Dennis on these occasions; they would invariably leave their clan and scramble up a cliffside to wander through the heather.

'All clear?' the cook asked from the doorway. She was in a better humour now.

'Yes. Cook do you know Dennis Maxted? He's twenty-three and has a black beard.'

'No.' Cook wiped her hands on her plump hips. ' 'Aven't seen any young fellows 'er this year with beards.'

Azette's shoulders drooped; she had

already asked the waitresses if they knew Dennis. Somebody *must* know him.

' 'Ere's a chair, Girl.' The cook surprised her by passing one through the doorway. 'Phyllis will bring a tea tray. Yer 'av ter snatch a break when yer can. Your back'll ache wors' before seven.'

★ ★ ★

That evening Azette was glad to flop into an armchair in Mandy's sitting-room, and watch television with her. Jane joined them soon after nine; she kicked off her best shoes and thrust her feet into Mandy's slippers.

'Andrew went out for the evening, so Aunt Monica drove me back.' She removed the pins from her red hair. 'I'll really let my hair down tomorrow evening,' she vowed. 'Mandy, we'll take Azette to the 'Silver Anchor'; possibly someone will know Dennis.' At the end of a documentary Jane said, 'The family have asked you to dinner, Azette.'

'That's very kind of them.'

'They must want to see for themselves who is sharing my flat. They suggested Tuesday as you'll be working over Easter. I'll be back at work then, but pack up at five-thirty.'

'I should be able to find a room next week as many holiday makers will have gone home.'

'No,' Jane insisted at once. 'It'll be fun having you with me — you must stay as long as you can.'

'Thanks, that'll be great, but I must pay my way.'

★   ★   ★

The next day, Saturday, passed very like the previous day for Azette, excepting that there were no surprises for her at the café; she knew how greasy dishes would get the better of her if she did not watch out, and knew how to humour Cook. She had hung on to the chair and wedged it between two cupboards.

On her arrival back at the flat, she soaked away her exhaustion in a hot bath. It was a gloomy damp evening, but the three girls threw raincoats over gay mini frocks and made their way down the promenade to the 'Silver Anchor'. Even Mandy made light of her troubles, although she was not looking forward to the next evening when her father and step-mother were driving from Dorchester to take her for a meal at an inn.

'It's lucky I don't show yet.' She threw back the front of her raincoat and smoothed her hand over her stomach.

'But you're going to show soon aren't you Mandy?' Jane pointed out. 'Your parents are bound to want to see you throughout the summer; you'll have to decide what to tell them.' They had turned into the High Street, and Jane softened when she noted the indecisive, bewildered look on Mandy's face; she hugged her arm reassuringly. 'Not to worry, I'll stand by you, but it would be easier if you'd tell me who the father is.'

Her friend's assurance cheered Mandy, and the girls entered the 'Silver Anchor' with stars in their eyes. Jane elbowed her way through a crowd of young people to the bar to order three Vodka and Limes; she was unsure if Mandy ought to drink, but, as she had given up smoking for the sake of the baby, she let the matter slide for the present. Azette noted that all the youths and girls called greetings to Jane, but when Jane repeatedly asked if anyone knew Dennis, the answer was always a shake of a head.

Azette grew increasingly despondent; people of Dennis's age ganged up in small towns like Tollbury, it was strange none of them had heard of him. Later she noticed two newcomers, wearing violet shirts and matching ties, were eyeing her speculatively. She asked:

'Excuse me, do you know Dennis Maxted?'

'Sorry, never heard of him,' replied one of the men. His hair scraped on his purple shirt collar as he turned to give his companion an insinuating look. He moved nearer to Azette to ask:

'Do you know anybody round here who we could score a joint from?'

Azette gaped at him, but quickly recovered. 'I'm a non-smoker,' she said in an icy tone before she moved away.

'You fool, what made you talk to them in the first place,' came an angry voice. Michael had detached himself from a group of young men, now he caught hold of Azette's wrist and swung her round to face him.

'How was I to know they were drug takers?'

'They're not. They are police in plain clothes out to trap somebody,' Michael glowered. 'It's safest not to talk to strange men.'

'I only asked if they knew Dennis.' Her mouth quivered. 'How many times must I ask that before I find him?'

'Now don't give up,' Michael told her hastily to ward off her tears. 'What sort of job would Dennis be doing?'

'He wasn't qualified; he could be

digging a hole in the road, delivering groceries or clipping deck chair tickets. He worked in a garage in St Helier for a while.'

'Now you've given me a lead — I'll make inquiries at all the garages in the district.'

★ ★ ★

Easter Sunday passed uneventfully for Azette. Michael had taken Jane for a day's drive in the country, and he was to take her back to supper with his parents who lived in a lovely house overlooking Tollbury Bay. As Mandy had joined her father and step-mother for the evening, the flat was very quiet. Azette felt homesick, and wrote a long letter to her parents.

The Bank Holiday crowd packed the café on Monday. In her haste to keep pace with the customers, Azette broke some plates in the morning, and was reprimanded sarcastically by Mrs Cornish for trying to juggle with them;

Azette thought of the future needs of Mandy's baby and remained calm. In the afternoon Cook put her head round the doorway to bawl:

'Quick. Drop everything Girl. Out. The police are 'ere. Someone 'phoned to say they 'ad planted a bomb in the café!' The woman waddled out of her kitchen as fast as her plump legs could carry her; she did not stop until she was halfway down the harbour.

Azette welcomed a break; she joined Phyllis, and the other waitresses on the sands where children were digging a moat round a large sand castle.

'As though anybody would bother to plant a bomb in harmless Tollbury,' laughed the first waitress. She pointed to a white speed boat which zoomed across the sea. It sent up a V of white foam as it skilfully wove in and out of the paths of slower moving vessels. 'Andrew Gordon is at the wheel of the Thompson's speed boat again.'

'Andrew Gordon,' repeated Azette.

'Is he the Andrew who owns Warren Farm?'

'That's right,' put in the second waitress. 'He's the most dishy bloke in Tollbury.'

'Yes,' sighed the third waitress. 'Andrew turns me on too.'

Phyllis wrinkled her nose thoughtfully. 'He is 'different'. Most girls don't get to know him properly because he doesn't come down here often, his farm takes up most of his time. They say he keeps to himself, and will look right through any girl who tries to chat him up.'

The girls spoke of other men until Mrs Cornish called from the foreshore that the bomb scare had been a hoax. The harbour was packed with excited holiday makers who had been speculating on the outcome of the arrival of the police car. Now it drove off, and was cheered by youths wearing black leather jackets; two of them shinned up a telegraph pole, the sea breeze moved their shaggy hair, and they reminded

Azette of bears at the zoo. A man skidded on an ice cream, and a small boy looked in astonishment at his empty ice cone. The café was filling quickly with those intent on spending the last of their holiday money before setting off for their long trek home. People queued for seats at the tables, and Azette was busy again at the sink.

'So this is where you work.' A long haired youth was grinning at Azette from the kitchen doorway; she wondered how he had managed to slip past Cook. He wore a faded blue T-shirt inscribed 'I'm a Virgin. How about you?' He moved confidently into the scullery to say, 'I followed you back from the beach.'

If Azette had not been so exhausted, she might have laughed at his cheek; now she stared at him speechlessly until a plump hand was laid on his shoulder.

'You've twenty seconds to take yer virginity out of 'ere — then I call th' police back,' Cook warned.

After this incident Azette was in no

mood to respond to the man wearing a white polo neck jersey who entered the yard and tapped on the scullery window. She ignored him, but soon he strode into the kitchen; he was very good-looking, she judged him to be in his late twenties. His hair was the colour of winter beech leaves, his mouth was wide and unsmiling, and his weather beaten features were bold. He made Azette think of the open country.

'Didn't you hear me rapping on the window?' he asked.

'Yes.'

'Then why ignore me?'

'I was busy.'

'So Mrs Cornish hasn't taught you to put the customers' needs first?'

'Neither has she taught me that the customer is always right.'

His eyes were holding hers now, she could not free herself. His silence reminded her of a dark night when she had walked down a lane near her farm; something had gripped her arm sound-lessly. Her fear of the unknown had held her as motionless as she was now. *Then* she had become aware that a partially broken branch of a young tree had fallen across her arm; her fear had vanished for the tree was an old friend. *Now* she was still afraid because she did not know what was behind this stranger's searching look. With an effort she turned away. The stranger watched as she emptied dirty water out of the washing-up bowl; she reached for a heavy new drum of washing-up liquid standing under the sink, he immediately grasped its handle and stood it on the draining board for her. He removed the stopper with one twist of his fingers, and poured some of the liquid into the bowl. Azette turned on the hot tap and minute soap bubbles rose and settled on the front of her overall. They appeared to fascinate the stranger.

'Sorry about this,' he apologised abruptly when a black and tan setter unexpectedly nosed his way between them. 'There was a water bowl in that cupboard last season. Ah, here it is. Boy

30

always has his drink outside.'

'Are you a friend of Mrs Cornish's?' asked Azette as the man filled the bowl with cold water.

'I'm an old customer.' (Azette had bent to pet the setter who was looking up at her knowingly.) 'My dog seems to have made a bigger hit with you than I have.'

Azette turned back to the sink without commenting, and the man accepted her action as a dismissal. When he had gone she swept up the lumps of damp sand which had fallen from his shoes, then she wiped the dog's paw marks from the floor, but she still felt their presence in the scullery.

Later Cook bawled from the doorway, 'Mr Andrew Gordon said I was to say 'Thank you', Girl.' She plonked the dog's water bowl on a side table.

3

'I'm beginning to doubt if Dennis is, or ever has been, in Tollbury,' Azette observed as she approached the 'bus shelter with Jane on Tuesday evening; they were to dine at Warren House.

'Don't develop a defeatist attitude,' advised Jane. 'You've only been here five days. Dennis might be on our 'bus.'

Dennis was not on their 'bus. Azette's spirits dropped as she took a seat by the window and looked intently at every young man in sight. This had become a habit now. She spotted Michael sitting at the wheel of his dark blue Daimler whilst an attendant filled its tank with petrol. As promised he had called on all the garages in the district, but nobody had even heard of Dennis. If Azette had found but one clue to prove that he was in the vicinity, she would have been happier.

'The family are a drag, Azette,' Jane uttered apologetically as the 'bus turned westwards along the coast road. 'Uncle George is a bachelor who has lived and breathed fossils since he retired from his University. Now he's just finished a book.'

'What is it called?'

'*Frolics with Fossils*, or something like that. It was started by Grandfather.'

'What are your aunts like?'

'Aunt May is the eldest. She never married, but I think she had a shady past which has kept her from becoming sour. She often lives in a dream world, then becomes awfully vague. Aunt Monica married a Lord, the sort whose title dies with him. When he popped it, she came back to Warren House. She's very lah-de-dah. Sometimes the three of them have great fun behaving like the quarrelsome brats they used to be. The old home is stiflingly Victorian, they persist in clinging to my grandparents' standards.'

The 'bus had left housing estates

behind, and was passing Andrew's farmland; it stopped at the entrance to a curving lane where Azette jumped out after Jane. A bedraggled lad sat on the verge; his shoes and bed-roll were amongst the weeds; he was spooning Mandarin Oranges from a can.

'He's the modern version of the tramp who used to call at Warren House to have his billy-can filled,' Jane whispered to Azette. 'Hey — you've dropped your tin opener,' she called in her friendly way.

'Ah, thanks.' The youth grinned as Jane picked it up from the road and passed it to him. 'It's the most valuable part of my kitchen equipment.'

'Have you come across Dennis Maxted on your travels?' Azette asked.

'Afraid not. Where does that lane lead to?'

'To my family home; but keep away or my aunt will set her ferocious dogs on you,' Jane commanded as her eyes danced merrily.

The lane, which was hedged with

hawthorn and brambles, was very stoney; Jane complained how painful it was walking in shoes with thin soles.

'They're not worth repairing; I wore them to keep the peace with Aunt Monica who thinks they're in 'good taste'.'

'Is that one of Andrew's pastures?' questioned Azette as she moved aside some young honeysuckle to peer over a hedge.

'Yes. He owns the land on the other side of the lane too. See — there's Warren House on the edge of that wood.'

The lane merged into the trees, and the pale evening sky was cut off until the girls came to the clearing where Warren House stood. It was sur-rounded by a trim garden consisting of well kept lawns and flower beds; the whole was enclosed by evergreen honeysuckle.

'My grandfather always had the window frames painted white, and the drain-pipes and front door painted black,' explained Jane on seeing Azette eyeing the painters' ladders leaning against the red brick walls of the house. Jane ran up the steps and pressed the front door bell. 'It's not done to let oneself in. Mr Curtis answers the door and keeps the house in order; his wife cooks.'

'It's a mild evening, Miss Jane,' Mr Curtis commented gravely as he held the door open. 'Your aunts are in the drawing-room.' He took the girls' coats solemnly.

A red and blue Turkey carpet ran from the door to a lofty sash window which afforded a good view of the sea. Mr Curtis bent to remove a clod of mud which lay on the highly polished lino alongside an enormous brass gong.

'Andrew usually carries part of his land with him,' Jane tittered as she led Azette along a short corridor where two white poodles waited outside the drawing-room door.

'Are those your aunt's ferocious dogs?' Azette smiled.

'Afraid so. Andrew has a splendid dog — a setter; he has shared the library with him since they came to live here. My uncle's study is over there.'

Jane opened the door of the feminine drawing-room, and the poodles trotted elegantly across a pink carpet to greet their beautifully groomed mistress. She stood by the french windows admiring the daffodils which nodded under a group of silver birch.

'Hi, Aunt Monica.' Jane waved her hand sideways.

'You are not an American Movie-Star, Jane,' Lady Monica shuddered.

Azette took in the cut of her exquisite black gown, her skilfully styled grey hair, her aristocratic nose and discreetly made up face. She inclined her head graciously when Jane introduced her new friend.

Then the girls turned to the fireside where a faded little woman sat in a Sheraton chair. Her bobbed grey hair was secured by a pink hair slide, and she wore a meaningless garment in mauve brocade; she was crocheting something purple, but laid aside the hook whilst greeting Azette in a twittering voice.

'What pretty hair you have child, so fair.'

'Thank you, Miss Marley, my father's family were all very fair.' On sensing the old lady waited for her to say something else, Azette added, 'What a wonderful sea view you have from here.'

'We have indeed. There's a way down to the beach where my brother collects fossils. My sister enjoys the garden whilst I like the wood. I bird-watch you know. Come and sit beside me and I'll tell you all about it.'

Whilst Miss Marley spoke at length about her hobby, Azette listened with half an ear to Lady Monica.

'Now Jane, I want you to be pleasant to Andrew. Wealthy young men don't grow on trees.'

'But Aunt, Andrew is as disinterested in me as I am in him,' Jane protested.

'Nevertheless you could arouse his

interest if you behaved in a more lady-like manner.'

'Oh there we go again,' Jane groaned in an aside.

'I beg your pardon?'

'I said that Andrew and I do not switch each other on.'

The door had been flung open, and Professor Marley growled, 'Those blasted painters — a landing window is stuck now. If they had done that in Father's time, he would have thrown them over the cliffs.'

The Professor was a stocky man dressed in a pre-war style grey suit; he had a boyishly pink complexion, a prominent nose and steely blue eyes; his striking yellow hair and yellow beard made him appear younger than he was. He approached Azette with an extended hand, and assured her he was delighted to meet her. In response to his questioning, she explained why she was in Tollbury.

Then came the booming of the gong. A white damask table cloth covered a mahogany table in the dining-room; its setting was similar to the settings the Marleys had favoured over fifty years ago, damask table napkins were laid on side plates, a bread basket was set precisely between a pair of cruets, and a cut glass water jug stood by two bottles of red wine. There were no flowers, the marble mantelpiece had been the place for those ever since Grandfather Marley had spotted a caterpillar swinging blissfully from a carnation above the butter pats.

'I suppose Andrew heard the gong,' the Professor growled as he seated himself at the head of the table facing his eldest sister. May had refused to relinquish this position even if Monica had returned home with a title. This haughty lady was seated on her brother's right hand, and Azette's place was laid on his left. Jane sat between her two aunts, she tugged impatiently at her over starched table napkin, then the brass door knob rattled.

Andrew wore a brown suit and a

cream shirt; Azette had to admit to herself that he did not appear so frightening when he smiled at everybody as he did now. When Jane introduced him to Azette, he behaved as though he had never met her before; perhaps he had forgotten her, she must have looked different with her hair tied back and her nose doubtlessly shining. Why was it that when she met his brown eyes, then glanced away, the gleaming silver on the table came to life and coloured lights quivered in the cut glass water jug. Glass and silver on the ugly mahogany sideboard shone and glittered too. Azette took up her soup spoon without being aware of doing so. Andrew sat next to her which caused her to feel unaccountably disconcerted.

After an exchange of conventional remarks, the Professor mentioned, 'Jane told me you were working in a café over Easter, Azette.'

'Yes Professor.'

'And what did you do there?' questioned Lady Monica in mounting horror.

41

'I was the washer-up.'

Lady Monica winced and blinked her eyelids distressfully. 'Whatever would your parents have said?'

Jane put in quickly, 'From what Azette has told me about her parents, I bet they'd have been glad that she insisted on taking the job over from somebody who was too ill to go through with it. That's so isn't it Azette?'

'Yes, that's so,' agreed Azette calmly.

Andrew's lips were twitching, and the laughter lines at the corner of his eyes had deepened.

'What did you do in Jersey Azette?' the Professor asked.

'I did secretarial work for five days a week in St Helier. At weekends I liked to go down to a beach, or to help around one of our farms.'

'And how many farms does your father own?' Miss Marley left one of her day dreams to ask.

'Only one. At Archriondel. It is to be handed down to my eldest brother. The farm at Portelet is my mother's. She will leave it to my younger brother who spends most of his time there now. This was agreed upon when my parents planned to marry.'

'They were lucky to have those two sons,' said the Professor. 'Andrew's family were placed in a similar position.'

Azette turned to Andrew questioningly.

He explained, 'My father's forebears came from Scotland. Five generations ago one of them bought a farm in Cornwall. This belongs to my father now, and will one day belong to my elder brother.'

'So you started up in Dorset?'

'It wasn't quite like that. My great-uncle inherited Warren Farm from his mother's family; when his son was killed in the war, he left everything to me, to even things up I believe.'

Andrew did not elaborate further. He accepted mustard from Miss Marley, and gave his attention to his roast beef. Azette thought he did not pursue the

43

subject of the ownership of farms because the farmhouse, which had been handed down to him as a trust, had been gutted by fire.

Jane was eager to tell anybody who was interested, how she had helped Michael put the final touches to his yacht on Easter Monday, and how she had at last agreed to crew for him.

'That's hardly a lady-like sport is it?' inserted Lady Monica. 'I've seen girls step out of small yachts looking like drowned rats.'

The Professor prepared to do battle; he set down his knife and fork with a clatter. Since childhood he had enjoyed putting his haughty sister in her place, besides he was very attached to Michael.

'Sailing is a clean healthy sport, and Michael is trust-worthy. When is he coming to fish with me again Jane? Tell him my boat is trim — all we'll need is bait.' He shot an impish look at Lady Monica, and was satisfied to see her throat work uncomfortably. 'But I apologize: 'bait' is not a good prelude to Mrs Curtis's Tipsy Cake.'

Andrew tactfully changed the subject by asking Azette if her name was French.

'Jersey-French. I was named after Grève d'Azette which is a place in Jersey. My mother was named Rozel after a Jersey bay, and my father and his sisters were named Geoffrey, Catherine and Anne after places on the East of the Island.'

Everyone encouraged Azette to speak of Jersey until the biscuits and cheese were disposed of. It was later in the evening, after six empty coffee cups had been replaced on a tray in the drawing-room, that Azette knew for a certainty that Dennis had recently passed close to Warren House.

4

It was incredible. Miss Marley had been moving uncomfortably in her Sheraton chair when her brother had growled:

'Stop fidgeting May. If you didn't hoard junk behind that damn silly cushion, you'd have more room.'

As Jane helped her aunt remove her hoard she enumerated: 'Item 1: Your skirt back from the cleaners Aunt May. Item 2: My lost silk square. Item 3: A dog's lead. Item 4: Those missing playing cards. Item 5: A man's grey jersey. Is it yours Uncle?'

'No, dear.'

'Yours Andrew?'

'No, Jane.'

'Then it must belong to Mr Curtis.' Jane held out the crew neck garment to reveal a rough L shaped darn in the elbow.

'No.' Azette had risen to her feet

slowly, her hands were trembling. 'It belongs to Dennis.'

'How can it?' cried Jane.

'Last time Dennis came to our farm he caught his elbow on a nail in a glass house. We were in a hurry to catch a 'bus I remember, so I made a temporary darn in red because there happened to be red wool threaded in a darning needle.'

'Hundreds of men wear grey jerseys,' said Lady Monica doubtfully.

'True. Aunt Simone had knitted one for Dennis's brother too — that's why they have name tapes.'

Jane examined the tape sewn at the back of the neck. 'Dennis Maxted,' she read before surrendering the garment to Azette.

Whilst the Professor was blessing his soul, Lady Monica looking curious and Andrew showing interest, Azette asked Miss Marley:

'Has Dennis been here Miss Marley?'

'Dennis? Who is he?'

'My cousin. Before dinner I was

saying I had come to Tollbury to find him.'

'Oh yes. No, he hasn't been to Warren House my dear.'

'Then how did you come to have his jersey Miss Marley?'

'I — can't think.'

'Please try. It means so much to me.'

'Let me see. I found it in the wood when I went to look at my owl's nest.'

'Where exactly in the wood?'

'On the tree that has fallen across the track. It was damp, I brought it home and aired it in front of a nice fire.'

'How long ago was that?' Azette kept her patience admirably.

'On the afternoon Monica went to Weymouth. When was that Monica?'

'The Friday before last.'

Azette sat down and clutched the jersey tightly. Less than two weeks ago its thick wool had retained the heat of Dennis's body. He must have rested on that tree which had fallen across the footpath, and had become lost in thought; when he went on his way, he had left the jersey behind. Azette became aware that everyone was watching her. She said:

'Tomorrow afternoon I shall go into the wood to find that fallen tree.'

'But your cousin won't still be sitting on it,' chriped Miss Marley brightly.

'What a damn silly thing to say, May,' the Professor uttered crushingly. He turned to Azette. 'That wood is no place for a young girl to wander about alone.'

'But I have to find out where that path leads.'

'It leads straight into a jungle,' warned Lady Monica. 'Andrew owns some of the land so he can tell you about that.'

Azette turned to him.

'That track meets another which twists and turns for over eight miles through a jungle as Lady Monica has said, Azette.' His brown eyes summed her up. 'I don't expect you're used to large areas of woodland in Jersey?'

'Not exactly.' Azette eyed Andrew

49

appealingly. 'Is there a village close by where Dennis could be staying?'

'No, there are only my farm cottages. I can assure you I'd know if Dennis had stayed in one of them.' He was obviously searching for something to say to cheer Azette. 'I'll ask at the police station tomorrow morning if Dennis called to see if his jersey had been handed in.'

The family volunteered helpful suggestions as to how Azette might find Dennis, until Jane asked Andrew:

'Why not have a bash at the piano?'

Jane knew Andrew would be happy to do so. He had lost his own piano in the farm fire, and the drawing-room piano was the only one he had access to. Jane delighted Lady Monica by standing beside Andrew; she sang snatches of popular melodies and ploughed through *The Skye Boat Song* because she knew it was a favourite of his.

When they were back in the flat Azette learnt this sugar sweet action of

Jane's had been prompted by the fact that the soles of her feet were tender after walking down the stoney lane in her thin shoes. She had reasoned that if she was especially nice to Andrew, he might offer to drive them home.

'I'm worried about Mandy,' Jane frowned after the girl had returned her record player.

'Haven't you any idea who the father is?'

'Mandy isn't the promiscuous type. She was in with a crowd of students, but they were back at universities when *it* happened. During that time she was only out with one man. She liked watching T.V. and sometimes came to the cinema with Michael and me; other times she'd baby-sit for Mrs Stewart, the lady she works for.'

'Who was the man Mandy went out with?'

Jane replaced some records in a rack. 'You'll think I'm bitchy when I say he was Andrew.'

'Oh,' exclaimed Azette bleakly. She

51

had not wanted it to be Andrew.

Jane continued. 'During the time *it* happened, Mandy went to Warren House several times to give Aunt Monica fittings — she'd been slimming and her frocks needed altering. Andrew often drove Mandy home because the winter 'bus service is poor. Sometimes they'd stop at an inn on the way back; I wouldn't know what else they did, but Andrew is supposed to be awfully sexy.'

'Most men are sexy given the chance,' Azette stated curtly. 'So you think Andrew could be the father?'

'Put it this way, if he isn't, I haven't a clue who could be.'

'Does Andrew know Mandy is pregnant?'

'She said she wouldn't tell the baby's father because it was her fault as much as his, and she said he'd had a lot of trouble recently. Well Andrew had trouble when he lost his farmhouse, and when his glamour widow married another man.' Jane wound up the clock on the mantelpiece prior to going to bed. 'Mandy is soft and self sacrificing.'

'But Andrew ought to be given the chance to help her,' Azette reasoned. 'Somebody ought to tell him she's in the family way.'

'If you think so, go ahead and tell him.' Jane's lips tightened. 'I never find much to say to Andrew.'

★ ★ ★

The following afternoon Azette, wearing her navy windcheater, slacks and walking shoes, entered Warren Woods. From under the ivy the moist soil gave off a pleasant odour; young leaves shivered in the soft sea breeze, and pines thrust dark green branches above lower growing trees. The track became grassy and divided; she turned seawards. Once a badger stood in her path, eyed her in astonishment, then scuttled into the undergrowth; Azette thought it early in the day for him to be about. The track was blocked by a fallen elm; this was where Dennis had left his jersey and where he had rested — here where the bark had peeled, and the trunk was smooth. Here she would think of him.

Where had Dennis been going when he had passed this way? Where had he come from? More important, where was he now? She must find him because he was a part of her, and perhaps he needed her help. When the sun came out and a bird sang in the tree above, Azette willed Dennis to appear, and strained her eyes to pierce the gloom where the trees grew thickly. Minutes passed, but there was no movement ahead; however Dennis might come from the other direction. She turned and gave a startled cry. A man sat on a mossy bank where primroses bloomed. She wanted him to have a pointed humorous face, strange flecked eyes, long black hair and a black beard. But he had a strong square face and copper-bronze hair.

'Did you follow me here Andrew?' Azette asked accusingly.

'No,' he responded evenly. 'But my conscience insisted I made sure you didn't walk over the cliffs or become lost in the jungle.'

'But why were you sitting there watching me?' Azette plucked at a piece of loose bark and peeled it off the tree trunk. Andrew had a way of making her feel uncomfortable.

'I didn't want to butt in on your thoughts. I guessed you were trying to conjure up Dennis,' Andrew surprised Azette by saying. 'You must love him very much to have come all this way to find him.'

'No, I don't love Dennis in the way you mean. You see we share great-grandparents and that, coupled with the fact that we paired off at family gatherings because we were the young-est, caused us to grow so close that we became like one person. Can't you understand how it was?'

'I'll understand better when I see Dennis.'

'And you *will* see him because I shall

find him soon. I felt inclined to give up when it seemed nobody in Tollbury had heard of him, but when I saw Dennis's jersey I knew it was only a question of time before I found him. I don't suppose you had any luck when you asked about him at the Police Station?'

'No; and nobody there remembered seeing anyone answering his description in Tollbury recently. Keep hoping.'

'I will.' Azette crossed the grassy track to stand in front of Andrew. 'If you could put me right about this track please, it must lead somewhere?'

'It leads to Faraway Lane which runs into the jungle about which I have already told you.' Andrew stood up and whistled. His black setter immediately bounded out of some bushes. 'If you want to learn the lay of the land, come up here, Azette.' She followed him up the mossy bank to where gorse grew amongst young pines. 'Now that you can see for yourself how close we are to the edge of the cliff, you won't stray from the track — I hope.' He pointed to the right. 'You can see how the land curves seawards, and how the woods form a jungle seemingly for ever.'

'What's on the far side of the jungle?'

'A large caravan site, then comes the next seaside resort. I expect Dennis merely came this way for a walk.'

Azette thought she detected impatience in Andrew's voice; he had given up time to her instead of attending to his farm. He was already ascending the primrose bank, and had turned to offer her his hand; but she hurried down between the clumps of primroses to the track unaided. He must have taken this as a snub.

'I don't think you like me very much do you Azette? You don't like me because I am not Dennis.'

She flushed. She had intended telling Andrew about Mandy's condition, but this did not seem the right moment. As they turned in the direction of Warren House, they heard a rustling, then Miss Marley pushed past branches of a dense hawthorn which snatched at her mauve cardigan. Andrew freed her before pressing through undergrowth in the direction of his pastures.

'I came here to see if the eggs are hatched in a nest over there.' Miss Marley took Azette's arm companionably. 'You must take tea with me. My sister has driven off somewhere, so I'll be glad of your company. Andrew usually has tea at one of the cottages, he's a very busy person. If he goes up to the hills he doesn't come home for luncheon either.'

Curtis had set out the tea things on a small table where the sun cast shadows by the french window. Whilst Miss Marley was pouring tea from the silver teapot (as her mother had done before her), her brother came in and slammed the door.

'I'm no typist, that is clear,' he bellowed.

'Then calm yourself with a good cup of tea, George,' suggested his sister mildly.

He snorted, but drew a chair to the

table and told Azette his troubles. The girl who had promised to type his manuscript had married instead. He had advertised in the local paper, but had received no favourable replies.

'Young women like working in towns, George,' May Marley reminded him. 'Now have one of these nice scones and you will feel better.'

'I want a typist — not a blasted scone.' But the Professor ate three scones, and drank two cups of tea which revived him. He watched Azette's calm movements as she spread strawberry jam on a scone; she was not a girl who became flustered easily. A well bred girl too. He asked her, 'Would you be looking for a job, Azette, now that your fight with dirty crocks is over?'

'Yes, I shall need a job if I'm to stay on in Tollbury.' Azette had put down her tea knife expectantly, she had guessed what the Professor was about to ask.

'Why not work for me? You'll find it child's play typing out my manuscript;

they tell me I write in a very legible hand.' He warmed to the idea. 'I'll pay you a generous wage. You could catch an early 'bus up in the mornings, take luncheon with us and leave here in time to catch the late afternoon 'bus back to Tollbury. You would have Saturday and Sunday free.'

Miss Marley clapped her small hands. 'That would be lovely George; don't you think so Azette?'

Azette supposed it could be lovely; she needed a well paid post if she was to stay on in Tollbury. Furthermore, since she had found Dennis's jersey, she had felt drawn to Warren House. He had passed close to it once, therefore he might well pass this way again.

'I will be very pleased to work for you Professor,' she told him smilingly.

5

The following morning Azette knocked at the door of the Professor's study promptly at nine o'clock. His room was neat and orderly. Glass cabinets displayed small fossils whilst larger fossils were ranged on a bench. There was a mahogany bookcase, and two green steel filing cabinets. The Professor sat at a table in the middle of the room; in the bay stood a typist's table which overlooked the front garden. Here Lady Monica was filling a small trug with white narcissi.

The Professor greeted Azette with relief. 'You should find your work interesting, Azette. First I must show you how to find your way around.' This proved simple for every container was methodically labelled so that it was practically impossible to go wrong. 'In here are photographs of my fossils taken by Michael; that young man is a first rate photographer, useful in his line of business, his father displays photographs of property outside his estate office.' He passed Azette a list of fossils written in his clear hand. 'I found these in the Blue Lias Beds, this will help you check your spelling.'

The typewriter was in good condition, and Azette worked industriously until the Professor plugged in an electric kettle.

'I trust you like Jasmine Tea, Azette? My father would say there was nothing like it for a mid-morning brew.'

Azette did not mention she had never tried Jasmine Tea; she thought it wisest to fall in with the Professor's habits. He conversed amicably whilst sipping his tea; Jane might describe him as a 'square', but he was just and kindly.

'Now the fine weather has come,' he observed contentedly, 'I must take my fishing tackle down to the boathouse. I suggest you accompany me after luncheon so that I can show you the way;

you are entitled to take a turn on the beach, or to explore the surrounding countryside, every day after luncheon; you youngsters need outdoor exercise.'

★ ★ ★

Luncheon at Warren House was conducted with almost as much old fashioned ceremony as was the evening meal. Azette was to find that dishes like macaroni cheese and fish pie were favourites, and there was always a stodgy pudding; she wondered how Lady Monica kept her figure trim until she noticed she never touched bread or potatoes. That day Andrew did not come in for lunch; he had driven to a market.

Miss Marley pecked at her food like a little bird. She told Azette she was crocheting a blanket for a Church Fête. She loved pretty colours — purples, emeralds, crimsons, sky-blues and glowing flames — she loved them all. Then Lady Monica graciously took over the conversation. She told Azette about the charities she supported; it was clear she enjoyed working tirelessly for them, and often held charity coffee mornings at Warren House. Azette privately summed up life in Warren House as being good and wholesome, but it was out of touch with present day life and Azette appreciated why Jane had wished to live in her own flat.

The Professor became alert when Mr Curtis set a rice pudding before Miss Marley; it was beautifully browned, and the Professor rubbed his hands together.

'I bags some skin.' He beamed like a schoolboy.

He was still beaming when he led Azette across the spacious garden behind Warren House. He pointed out the flower beds, the rose borders edged with paving stones, the bold plantings of shrubs which acted as wind breaks, the vegetable garden (where the gardener was working) and the potting shed which was screened by a trellis.

'See, Azette, those *Cupressus Macro-carpa* were planted near the cliff edge to ward off the wild winds, and behind them, on the sea side, is that wattle fencing to keep sea salt away. Now here is the gate to the lane.'

This steep lane had been kept in good repair with tarmac, and terminated at a slipway which ran down to a foreshore of blue and grey pebbles.

'Is this where you found all the fossils Professor?' Azette asked.

'Some of them, but like my father, I have made excursions to other beaches.'

The Professor unlocked his boathouse whilst Azette crossed to the water's edge. She opened the bag of stale bread Miss Marley had pressed on her, and threw some in the direction of gulls who rested on the calm sea. They left the water with a quick flapping of wings; they shrieked and fought each other for the bread, tried to catch some in their beaks and, when failing to do so, swooped back on to the sea for it. When the bread was gone, Azette popped a piece of bladder wrack absently until a boat, which resembled a small barge, came slowly past. Two indistinct figures waved to her, and she waved back. The gulls rose and circled overhead, and she imagined they cried 'Dennis, Dennis, Dennis.' The waves rolled up to her, the large ones moved quickly, the smaller ones slowly and the gulls cried, 'Dennis, Dennis,' again.

'That's Billy Preston's barge,' the Professor told Azette on joining her. 'He can't come too near the shore, hidden reefs separate many of these coves.'

'Is Billy Preston the pebble picker?'

'Yes, he's been at it for years so it must be profitable; one needs a strong back for it.'

'Where does he find the pebbles?'

'Find them!' The Professor laughed heartily. The sea breeze ruffled his yellow hair and beard until they resembled a chick's down. 'That should present no difficulty along this coast-line. But actually permission is needed from the Council for rights to pick on a certain beach, they make a charge for that naturally. The pickers grade the pebbles into two sizes, and pack them into polythene bags.'

'But what are the pebbles used for?'

'They are ground to make scouring powder; a lorry collects them from the harbour and drives them to a factory.'

As Azette re-crossed the sands with the Professor, she gave a backward glance at the barge. The gulls followed it now. They cried poignantly, 'Dennis, Dennis, Dennis.'

* * *

The days passed pleasantly for Azette; she would have been content, but for the fact that she had not yet come upon another clue which could prove that Dennis was staying in the district. She devoted her evenings, and weekends, to searching for him; she would accompany Jane to different bars — surely Dennis must frequent one of them; she would speak to the girls she encountered in cafés — Dennis liked pretty girls, surely he must have chatted one of them up, and she would ask assistants in the shops if they remembered serving Dennis. But nobody had any recollection of seeing him.

'I think you're the sort of girl who never lets go when she gets her teeth into anything,' remarked Andrew bluntly when they were discussing her search for Dennis at the lunch table one day.

'Azette knows when she's on to a good thing apparently,' the Professor inserted jestingly. 'May, your beads will soon be stuck to your plate,' he shot down the table at his sister whose ivory beads swung too near the hot syrup she had poured over her suet roll.

There followed a session of light bickering between the family, Andrew grinned tolerantly and was soon talking farming with Azette. This was their only common ground at present.

'I suppose you've seen my Friesians?' he asked when Azette spoke of the rich milk yielded by her father's pedigree Jersey herd.

'No. I've never been over your farm.'

He eyed her in surprise. 'Why not?'

'I don't like trespassing on a farmer's land.'

'Rot. I'll show you round after we leave the table.'

★ ★ ★

'This is well drained land,' Andrew pointed out as he led Azette along the edge of a field. 'We'll be sewing mangolds here.'

'I suppose you have a four year rotation?'

'No a six year. Oats, potatoes, wheat, roots, barley and hay.' He grinned at Azette banteringly. 'I've never talked about mangolds and turnips with a girl before.'

'But I came walking with you so that we could discuss farming,' she reminded him. 'You've only farmed here two years haven't you?'

69

'Yes, I carried on with my Uncle's plans for rotation.' He looked across to the distant hills. 'Does your father go in for sheep?'

'No he hasn't sufficient pasture land; it is so precious that Jersey farmers must stake their cattle to one patch of grass at a time to avoid wastage. Where are your sheep?'

'Up on those hills; it is rich downland, they can graze off short grass. They are Dorset Horn Sheep — a special breed.'

'I've not heard of them before.'

'Then I'll drive you up to see them one day.' He opened a pasture gate, the new spring grass was a lush green. 'Well, what do you think of my Friesians?' he asked.

It was nearing milking time so they were waiting by the far gate; Azette approached them eagerly, she wanted to compare the black and white herd with the small fawn Jerseys she was used to. She regarded their full udders critically.

'They are exceptionally good milkers,' Andrew impressed upon her.

'Yes, I can see that but — ' Azette looked round the broad pasture with a lost expression. 'Everything seems so vast after our little pastures, I just can't take it all in.' She wanted the security of snug leafy lanes, and of small fields where potatoes and tomatoes grew. 'Where do your cows sleep in the winter, Andrew?'

He took her up a lane to the farmyard. He introduced her to Posser the cowman who had such a pronounced Dorset accent that she found him difficult to understand. He showed her the large airy cowshed and the milking parlour, then she followed Andrew to the shed where the farm implements and machinery were housed.

'Green is out with the tractor now. A good tractor can take care of all sorts of jobs. Plough, cultivate, harrow, drill, roll, distribute manure, and rake — fetch and carry too, but then you'll know all about that Azette.'

They next inspected the Dutch barn which Andrew said was a more economical method of roofing ricks than thatch. Afterwards they passed a pair of stone cottages; their gardens were given over to vegetables, excepting for small oblongs of grass across which laundry lines were slung.

'Do these cottages belong to your farm Andrew?'

'Yes. Posser has the one with the swing in his garden, he has two children, and Green, who is newly married, has the other.' Andrew whistled, and Boy ran up to him from a gateway. 'He's buried a bone in Mrs Green's garden, she lets him dig it up when he fancies it.'

Azette thought that Mrs Green's garden must be a happier place for Boy than was the formal garden at Warren House. Then she saw the ruins of the old farmhouse in an untidy garden. Andrew paused and looked over the cob wall where pennywort and ivy leaved toadflax grew between the stones.

'That is all that was left of the house,' he said dejectedly. 'Come inside.'

Andrew threw open the garden gate, and Azette followed him unhappily. She watched a mallard drake waddle past, and step through a doorway into what must have been the kitchen; against a shady wall a duck sat on her nest. Andrew had picked up a long iron hook which had been half concealed by weeds.

'What is that for?' she asked.

'It's a grappling-iron. It is an old fire fighting implement for dragging burning thatch off roofs. Well, it was no use on that night.' She sensed his deep sorrow; the garden felt too sad to have more unhappiness added to it. He dropped the hook back into the weeds and said bitterly. 'You must have heard how a chimney caught fire, and how the thatch was blazing before Posser spotted it from his bedroom window. There was not much left by the time the fire brigade arrived.'

'How terrible. I am so very sorry.' Azette would have spoken as gently to anybody under the circumstances.

'Don't trouble to be sorry,' he responded roughly. 'It was my own fault for leaving such a large fire in the grate when I was staying out so late.'

Before he could condemn himself further by telling her he had stayed out late to share a widow's bed, Azette stated calmly:

'Miss Marley told me she had seen Jackdaws dropping sticks and straw into your chimney, they were starting to build a nest. When a large fire was lit, that dry stuff would have been enough to send sparks flying. They would have set both the chimney and the thatch on fire.'

'Perhaps,' he agreed in a voice which sounded somewhat comforted.

Azette was glad he had not mentioned the widow; their past relationship was something he was entitled to keep to himself even if the gossips had made

74

'hay' out of it. Many women must be attracted by Andrew's strong personality, and by the bold lines of his features and the cut of his unusual russet brown hair. Had Mandy fallen for his charms? If he was the father of her child, as Jane half suspected, he was entitled to be given the chance to do something about it before he could be condemned. Azette's brow puckered as she wondered how she could get this matter across to him without implying that he might be involved. Then, unknowingly, Andrew made it simple for her to do so.

'You look so worried Azette. I told you not to feel sorry for me.'

'It wasn't that Andrew.' She met his eyes keenly. 'I have been thinking about Mandy. She is pregnant, and Jane and I want to help her, but she won't tell us who the father is.' It was out now. She shut her lips tightly, and watched for Andrew's reactions whilst never for an instant taking her eyes off him.

Surprise slid into his brown eyes, compassion followed and then concern.

'That is a shame, a great shame,' he voiced at last. 'Mandy is too young and sensitive to have to go through that sort of thing alone. If there is anything I can do at any time to help, you must let me know.' Andrew's dog caused a diversion then by snapping at a crane-fly. He was sitting where the front door of the farmhouse had once been. 'Thank God Boy was with me on the night of the fire.'

Something about the way in which Andrew bent to pat his dog made Azette feel certain that he could not be callous in his treatment of a girl as sweet as Mandy. She left him alone with his dog, and tested a rusty pump the base of which was concealed by bluebells. It did not work. How quiet it was; it was the silence of a home which had suffered, but had not lost hope. She thought it would be a pity if Andrew did not soon have the farmhouse rebuilt. She moved on and pictured how the garden would look when cleared of weeds, and she pictured how breezes might move the curtains at the open windows of the new farmhouse. Would Jane ever have the right to draw those curtains?

When Andrew crossed to her, she smiled at him pensively; he clasped her hand and they went to the gate together.

'Everyone goes through a rough patch, now it's Mandy. But if we press on we must come out of it sooner or later,' he said.

6

'If we climb that hill, Azette, we can have tea at the Tollhouse Café,' Jane suggested the next Saturday afternoon. 'We could ask if they have seen Dennis; a pity they didn't know of him at the library as you said he liked reading.'

Since morning a mist had hung low over the hills, and cars passed the girls with their headlights on. The Tollhouse had been built when only one road led to Tollbury; it was a thatched eighteenth century building, a board in its porch listed the tolls due for various types of horse-drawn vehicles and cattle.

'You'll be able to compare Dorset Cream Teas with Jersey Cream Teas, Azette,' Jane remarked when they were settled at a small table close to a diamond-paned window. 'That's Mrs Preston at the counter, she's the wife of Billy the pebble picker. In small

78

places like Tollbury nearly everybody you meet is related to somebody you have already met, or heard of.' Mrs Preston was a comfortable looking woman with iron grey hair; when she came to take the girls' order, Jane asked her, 'Do you know a fellow called Dennis Maxted, Mrs Preston? He's twenty-three and has longish black hair and a black beard. My friend is looking for him.'

Mrs Preston turned to Azette. 'I'm sorry, Miss, but I've never heard of him, or seen anybody here who looks like that. We get very few young people here, they go to the cafés down town. Most of our customers are older and come by car, that's why we had our car park enlarged.'

'Oh well, it was a try anyway,' declared Jane as Mrs Preston left them. She leant back in her rush chair, pressed her feet against the bar under the table and regarded Azette hopefully. 'I bet you won't mind doing me a good turn next Saturday morning Azette. I bet you won't mind crewing for Michael.'

'But I thought you had promised to.'

'I had, but there's this chap who had a tooth out yesterday afternoon, he was in such a panic that I had to hold his hand. He said he wanted to repay me by driving me to Bournemouth next Saturday.'

'That's not fair to Michael.'

'But I shall tell him whom I'm going out with, I never lie to Michael.'

'That's something anyway.'

Jane ignored that comment. 'If I don't spread myself around Michael will have the wrong idea, he'll ask me to marry him or something.'

Jane looked at Azette so appealingly that she recalled how she had taken her in unquestioningly on her arrival at Tollbury. 'O.K. I'll crew for Michael.'

Jane made haste to close the matter before Azette changed her mind; when she took the bill to the counter she told her, 'There's a cute parrot in the courtyard through that door, Azette, you ought to see him.'

The mist in the courtyard came and went mysteriously, but the parrot was comfortably installed in an alcove by the entrance to the boiler house. He had a scarlet head and wings and a blue breast, and he squawked harshly when Azette tried to converse with him. Something made her look across the cobbled courtyard to where a light shone from an uncurtained window on the ground floor. Through the mist she saw that the room was an artist's studio; she felt compelled to move closer to it. It was furnished sparsely, an easel stood close to a second window, paints and brushes were on a table and oil paintings, framed and unframed, hung on the walls.

'Azette, Azette,' Jane was calling her.

And so Azette recrossed the cobbles, and left the café with her friend. She was very thoughtful as they descended the hill past gardens where tulips and grape hyacinths bloomed. She was remembering how, before he left school, Dennis had turned his bedroom into a studio. It always smelt of turps, and he had been so keen on painting that she had thought he was going to take it up seriously. But later his father had forbidden him to waste his time for he had examinations ahead; and so canvases, paints and easel had disappeared from Dennis's room, it became a study, and the smell of turps never returned.

'Does Billy Preston paint?' Azette asked Jane.

'Great heavens no.'

'There was a studio overlooking that cobbled yard. Do the Prestons have a lodger?'

'Only Terry Guard.'

'Who is he? But oh I remember, he's Billy's crew.'

'That's right,' assented Jane. 'Look, the mist is thicker down the town now.'

Azette thought of the mists which sometimes pressed inland at Jersey, and she thought of the numerous times she had passed through these mists with Dennis. Their lives had been too linked together for them not to meet again.

★ ★ ★

Next Saturday the weather was glorious, Jane had left the flat in such a hurry to drive to Bournemouth with her new friend that, when Azette waved good-bye to her from the bedroom window, a cloud of her talcum powder had not settled. Azette replaced the lid of the perfume bottle which Jane had left perched precariously on her bedpost, then, she put on Dennis's grey jersey over her denim jeans and left the flat to meet Michael. He was waiting for her on the promenade.

'Are you sure you can stand up to that sea?' was the first thing he wanted to know.

'Of course I can. I've been out in boats as far back as I can remember.'

'Good of you to stand in for Jane.'

'I'm glad to help you Michael, but

you do let Jane walk all over you — a pity.'

'I'm a fool, but I won't have to put up with it much longer; in a few months I'll be opening a new Estate Office for Dad in Poole. It'll be quite a step up for me.'

'Good for you. I expect you'll be able to sail from Poole?'

'Yes.'

'And you'll not be able to see Jane often?'

'I could on Sundays I suppose, but it may be best to make a clean break if I'm not going to get anywhere with her.'

'How far did you hope to get?' Azette added hurriedly, 'I mean did you want to marry her?'

'It could have been a good idea if she had decided to settle down at last; I can count on my father helping me out with a mortgage. I could find a nice little house near the coast.' He gave Azette a meaning look. 'About time you thought of settling down too Azette, maybe you will when you meet up with your cousin.'

'Oh no, things won't be like that between us,' laughed Azette lightly. She felt light-hearted that morning, she sensed it would not be long now before she met up with her cousin.

'What will you do when you find Dennis? Go back to Jersey with him?'

'I can't do that until the end of the summer, it will take that long for me to finish the Professor's manuscript; I promised him that whether I found Dennis or not, I would stay here until I had completed typing his book.'

They turned down the harbour's slip-way where Michael helped Azette into a life-jacket before they pushed his small yacht into the harbour which was alive with other colourful sailing craft. Michael's sail was a startling yellow, and he had repainted the name *The Swift* in gold on the white hull. Soon they were in the open sea where Azette moved from one side of the small yacht to the other according to which way

Michael wished to turn. When she thought she had the hang of it, he warned her:

'You'll have us over next time if you do that.'

'That's what you threatened last time,' she responded calmly. 'But we're still afloat.' Her jeans were swamped, but she had come prepared for a wet passage.

'You lack any sense of timing, Azette,' Michael exploded. 'Now we're going to steer a straight course — even you can't go wrong.'

They headed towards the distant shore where cliffs towered above isolated pebble beaches. One of the cliffs soared to a peak, a cloud hung low on its summit and Azette thought it looked like a smoking volcano.

'If we carry on we'll be on a reef,' shouted Michael bursting in on her musings.

Azette's heart sank at the thought of assisting him to turn *The Swift*; she was only familiar with motor boats and rowing boats.

Michael bellowed, 'Keep your feet in the toe straps or you'll be in the sea.' However after they had manoeuvred their way between other craft, and sailed back into the harbour, Michael's good humour returned. 'Sorry I lashed out at you Azette. Actually you did damn well for a beginner.'

'Dennis, Dennis, Dennis,' shrieked some gulls.

Azette followed their flight until they hovered over the pebble picker's barge which had docked whilst they were out at sea. Billy Preston and Terry Guard were stacking polythene bags of pebbles on the quayside. Azette's heart raced wildly, she leapt out of the boat and ran up the slipway. 'Sorry, can't stop,' she cried on banging into Andrew who was ready to help Michael trundle *The Swift* back to the boat park. Andrew watched with Michael as Azette laid her hand on Terry Guard's arm. Everything happened surprisingly quickly after that. Azette introduced her cousin to Andrew and Michael, and offered a hasty explanation.

'Dennis has done away with his beard and long hair, and changed his name.' She added an excited farewell, 'See you — '

'See you,' returned Michael.

Andrew gave a short laugh, but said nothing.

Azette flashed her cousin a dazzling smile, 'Well, we've lots — '

' — to catch up on,' finished Dennis. 'So, see you chaps — '

' — around,' finished Azette.

For a moment the couple appeared to be taking their bearings, Azette's cheeks glowed, her fair hair hung in damp tangles over the shoulders of Dennis's grey jersey, and her wet jeans clung to her legs. Dennis was wearing faded denims and an old pullover of Billy's. His strange flecked eyes were restless, and his body seethed with impatience as though he could not wait to express his emotions. His animation was passed on to Azette. Without another word, they leapt off the slipway on to the wet sands.

Andrew and Michael watched as they waded through the harbour shallows, raced across the shingle with a stray dog barking at their heels, dodged through a game of football, splashed amongst waves up to their thighs, slithered on rocks and climbed over a breakwater. Then they were out of sight, but clearly nothing was going to stand in the way of their elated progress.

'Do you think they always carry on like that when they are together?' grinned Michael. 'Azette looked a different person didn't she?'

'She did,' Andrew agreed. 'What an odd re-union. They seemed to be trying to run back into their childhood days. Oh well, let's see to your boat, then we'll have a drink.'

★ ★ ★

Azette and Dennis had come to rest on an isolated rock, sea spray spattered

89

them, but the tide was going out.

'Now that I've told you how I came to be in Tollbury, Dennis, and told you how I came to be wearing your jersey, it's your turn. Begin — '

' — at the beginning. Right. I guess you know that I left home because I couldn't stand Dad's attitude any longer. When I refused to go to University, he crushed everything I wanted to do. He almost sapped my confidence in myself — but not quite. Not even you knew that when he insisted I gave over wasting time painting, I only pretended to obey him; I cleared my paints out of my room and carted the lot round to Mark's place; he had offered me a corner of his studio. I worked there whenever I could and he both taught and encouraged me. Later he said I ought to be attending an art school in London. So I drew out the cash Grandfather had left me, and cleared off.'

'Without saying good-bye to me.'

'How on the hell could I ever say

good-bye to you? Anyway we're not the type to have sentimental farewells are we? I showered you with post-cards of the sights of London didn't I?'

'One of the Tate, one of the National Gallery and a few Van Goghs to be exact,' Azette smiled forgivingly. 'How did you make out at the art school?'

'Surprisingly well; in fact I was soon selling my stuff.'

'Then why are you reduced to pebble picking?'

'Oh that — it pays for my board and the sea air keeps me fit, I was beginning to feel stifled in London. I spent last Christmas with an art student whose home is in Tollbury. We both returned to London in January, but I *had* to come back to Tollbury, I suppose I sensed I could paint happily here. The Prestons let me have a studio at the back of their café. I spend all my spare time painting oils for the exhibition I intend to hold this summer, that's why you haven't seen me around the town.'

'And when will you go back to

Jersey? Your mother has missed you more than you can know.'

'I'm sorry about that. And Dad?'

'I guess in his secret heart he realises he made a mistake treating you like that. Won't you go home Dennis?'

'I will if my exhibition is a success.'

'It *has* to be.'

7

'Ship Ahoy mate!' squawked the parrot from its perch when Azette entered Dennis's studio the next afternoon.

'Ship Ahoy mate,' Dennis added his greeting cheerfully.

He stood before his easel selecting paint from his palette. Azette stepped back to view his canvas. The parrot was a tatty bird, his feathers were dull and he could be moulting — or perhaps he always looked that way. But the parrot on the canvas was a gorgeous bird; its scarlet head and wings gleamed like shot silk, and the blue feathers on his breast had warmth and depth; its eyes glittered.

'That's absolutely great Dennis,' Azette cried happily. 'But then I remember how when I saw your work years ago in St Helier you'd make everything look that much more alive.'

Her heart raced with pride for her cousin. 'You have improved.'

'Glad you think so.'

'I do although I'm no judge of art.' She turned away. 'Now I'll amuse myself whilst you carry on. You promised you'd not stop work for me.'

Azette paced slowly round the studio; she studied all Dennis's paintings thoughtfully. She was not qualified to criticize them, but Dennis's work was as alive, and as vibrant as himself; Azette rightly sensed that it was first class. Her spirits rose, she felt certain that Dennis had done the right thing when he had gone his own way, even if it had meant running off from his home.

'If you look through those folders stacked in the corner, Azette, you'll see the hundreds of drawings I've done. They are dated from the time when I moved my gear into Mark's studio. He said if I kept everything I drew, I'd be able to look back and see how I'd improved.'

Azette sat quietly on a wicker chair to look through the folders, until Dennis scraped his palette clean, and said, 'I can't do any more until the paint is dry.'

'What made you change your name?' This was one of the many questions Azette had not yet asked.

'I wanted to start a new life, so I flipped through a book and picked out the words 'can *Terry guard* something or the other.' I've always liked the name Terry.'

'Did you use that name to sign the paintings you sold in London?'

'Yes.'

'You haven't signed any of these yet. Won't you use your real name for the Exhibition? Uncle Adrian is far more likely to unbend if you do.'

'I'll think about it,' replied Dennis curtly.

'What a pity your father wouldn't face up to the fact that, unlike Sophia and Justin, you hadn't inherited his love for healing.'

'It is a pity. Uncle Maurice fell out with Grandfather for more or less the same reason. The old chap could not understand why Uncle Maurice wanted so desperately to write; it was years before Grandfather even read one of his books — they were all best sellers too.'

'Somewhere in your family there must have been a creative urge.'

'Mother's people were corn merchants and farmers. The Maxteds were given to science and medicine, but there were all sorts of people in Grandmother Maxted's family — the Renoufs, your father's family. Those who didn't farm were soldiers, smugglers, poets and potters.'

'I like to think that we share our Renouf great-grandfather, Dennis. But don't forget that Mum had Renouf blood too because one of her ancestors married a Renouf girl who was the twin of a Renouf boy. But then, in the old days, so many Jersey families were twice related as you and I are.'

They talked on about their Renouf

ancestors, who could have passed much of themselves down to them both, until Dennis took up his brushes.

'Wish there was a sink here. I have to wash my brushes in my bedroom wash-basin. Shan't be a sec'.'

Azette crossed to the large window which was responsible for turning the room into such a good studio. On the far side of a gravel path an expanse of moorland stretched as far as she could see. She threw open the window, and leaned out eager for the sweet scent of heather. It was a beautiful spring afternoon, the sky was clear blue and a light wind carried whisps of cloud along. Gorse was in bloom and blackberry bushes were in leaf. This kind of country had always spelt freedom for Dennis and her. It must have spelt freedom to the parrot too.

'Hey — close that window for heaven's sake,' Dennis yelled from the doorway.

Even as he spoke there was a flapping of scarlet wings as the parrot left its perch, and flew out of the window over Azette's head. She faced Dennis in horror.

'I thought he was chained to his perch.'

'And I thought you'd have had more sense than to open the window with him in the room.' Dennis hastily flung his brushes on a table. 'After him. He's priceless.'

'How priceless is he?' Azette panted as they ran through the heather in the wake of the parrot.

'He has no money value you idiot; I meant in terms of affection. I'll never have the courage to face the Prestons if he's lost.'

His words caused Azette to run even faster over the springy soil, her hair flew back from her face which had taken on such a determined expression that Dennis had to laugh.

'You've forgiven me then?' she asked breathlessly.

'Yes, I've forgiven you.'

They chuckled together as they

pushed past some prickly gorse, and skirted an outcrop of rock. The parrot was out to plague them; he would alight on a tree, or a rock, a short way ahead of them, but when they were about to close in, he would take off again.

'You'd think they would have had his bloody wings clipped,' Dennis gasped. Now he too was becoming short of breath.

The parrot continued to keep just so much ahead of them. They bounded through young bracken, chased through couch grass, and avoided rabbit droppings only to trip over hummocks. At last the bird settled on the topmost branch of a silver birch; through a screen of half formed leaves, they could see it stretching its neck to peer down at them.

'I'll climb up and grab him,' Dennis declared.

A sharp crack echoed over the moorland as a branch snapped off the tree, and Dennis landed amongst the heather.

'Don't burn the toast,' the parrot squawked.

'Are you hurt?' Azette bent over her cousin. 'Or only winded.'

'I was winded *before* climbing that tree, imbecile.' Dennis sat up, then stood gingerly. 'Nothing broken.' He sat down. 'We'll have to wait for that damn bird to take off again.'

'Good. I could do with a breather.' Azette threw herself down on the heather beside her cousin. 'Why is it that when we're together something usually goes wrong Dennis?'

'Can't say. We'd better keep our eyes on the parrot. If he flies into that wood we may lose him.' Dennis lay flat on his back and kept his eyes focused on the parrot. 'Be ready to put on a spurt if he ruffles a feather.' He pushed his dark hair off his forehead.

'What made you cut your hair short and give up the beard?' Azette asked.

'I never liked myself that way.'

'Then why — ?'

'Didn't I shave? To annoy — '

' — your father of course.'

'You always knew me too well. Fancy you leaving home to look for me Azette.'

'You were away for so long Dennis — ' She could not explain what it had meant to her to be parted from him.

Never before had she needed to suppress her feelings for him. Now her thoughts seemed to be hovering in the air like the heath butterfly who fluttered uncertainly above them. Azette wanted very much to know if Dennis felt anything more than a cousinly regard for her? But he said nothing. The butterfly's blue wings quivered purposefully now; it flew down between them and came to rest on a yellow Needle-Whin. Dennis and Azette watched its movements and, as though aware they had taken their eyes off him, the parrot gave a squawk.

'Tea or coffee?'

Dennis swore when scarlet wings flapped overhead. He sprang to his feet and helped Azette up. They sighed with relief as the bird flew straight back to the Tollhouse.

* * *

After Dennis and Azette had enjoyed a substantial tea, to which they helped themselves in the café kitchen at Mrs Preston's invitation, Dennis surprised his cousin by driving an open sports M.G. to the side door.

'Only second hand,' he explained. 'But paid for.'

'Bought out of pebble pickers wages?'

'No out of some of the paintings I sold in London.' There was a terrific roar as Dennis started up the engine, and turned on the road which ran down to Tollbury. 'I need this car so that I can push off into the country to paint whenever the mood takes me. Also I haunt auction sales in search of frames which I can do up for my exhibition.'

When they entered Jane's flat, Michael was relaxing in a deep armchair in the sitting room. He greeted them with:

'You're just in time. Jane's making coffee.'

Jane put her red head round the doorway to ask laughingly, 'Black or white Terry Guard? Because don't expect me to get out of the habit of calling you that. If you hadn't changed your name, I'd have produced you for Azette right away.' Jane was in a good mood when Azette joined her in the kitchenette. 'I've spent a super after-noon with Michael.' She shut the door so that her voice would not carry into the sitting-room. 'The drive to Bournemouth yesterday was a flop; John was such a bore. I nearly hitched back.'

'Then all that scent and talc was wasted,' Azette smiled. 'If you keep Michael dangling on a string much longer you'll lose him for good. You're not the only attractive girl in Tollbury. Michael has good prospects now that he's going to open up the Poole office for his father; fellows of his age usually think of settling down.'

'But I don't want to settle down yet.'

'You're twenty-three, and there's no future in fooling around with a crowd; even they will eventually marry and younger ones will take their places — then you'll be an outsider.'

Jane tossed her head, opened the door and carried the coffee tray into the sitting-room where Michael and Dennis were in good spirits. The girls curled up at opposite ends of the settee, and left the talking to them — sometimes laughing uncontrollably at their jokes, other times lost in their own thoughts. Laughter was cut off abruptly when there came a tapping at the door.

'Sorry, I thought Jane and Azette were alone,' Mandy apologized shyly as she put her hands up to the towel which was wound turban wise round her head; her plum dressing-gown hid any signs of her pregnancy. 'Please excuse my wet hair, I came for my dryer.'

'Don't apologize Mandy. You make a grand White Rajah.' Michael sprang to his feet and gave a mock bow.

Mandy's melancholy dark eyes passed from Michael's familiar countenance to Dennis's merry face. Azette thought she looked paler than ever then, if that was possible.

Dennis's look of wonderment at Mandy's arrival changed to one of intense excitement as he stood up with one of his quick movements.

'Mandy! The girl with the eyes,' he exclaimed.

'I did not think you would ever come back to Tollbury,' Mandy said softly.

'After a few weeks in London, I decided that I could paint better in a peaceful place like Tollbury.' Dennis was staring hard at Mandy who was obviously embarrassed. 'When we met at that party, I said you had the most paintable eyes I'd ever seen. I must paint your portrait. When are you free? Tomorrow?'

'Well I — ' Mandy's eyes swam with secret emotions. 'I have a job you see.'

'You don't work on Sundays?'

'No but sometimes my father comes to take me for a drive.'

Mandy reminded Azette of a gentle woodland creature who has been caught in a trap. In an endeavour to rescue her she said:

'I'm sorry I forgot to return your dryer Mandy. It's in the bedroom. I'll fetch it.'

When Azette came back Dennis was asking ' — and where do you hang out Mandy?'

'Across the landing.'

Mandy held out her hand for the hair dryer, but Dennis intercepted her. 'You must not plug it in with wet hands. I'll fix it for you.'

Mandy left the room silently with Dennis following; Azette thought it was taking him an unnecessarily long time to plug the hair dryer in. When at last he returned he was laughing to himself.

'Must buzz off now, have to be up at the crack of dawn tomorrow to pick pebbles. Thanks for the coffee Jane.'

'You're welcome any time Terry

— Dennis, but before you go, do tell me how your grey jersey came to be in Warren Woods?'

'I'd been working on the beach with Billy when I spotted an overgrown path leading up the cliffs to the jungle above. I've always enjoyed a difficult climb, and Billy said he'd handle the barge if I wanted to see if there was anything paintable at the top.'

'And was there?' Jane asked.

'No. It isn't always easy to find a subject which I desperately want to paint. Sometimes I nearly give up hope, then I'll spot something which I *must* put on canvas — something as expressive as Mandy's eyes.'

8

The next week the weather worsened, gigantic waves threw up flotsam and jetsam of all descriptions. Hitherto it had been Jane who would be on the alert whenever the girls heard warning rockets to summon the crew to the lifeboat station; but, when there was a rough sea, Azette would fear for Dennis who went out almost daily with Billy.

On Tuesday there was mounting excitement in Warren House. This was one of Lady Monica's charity mornings, and every lady in the neighbourhood who was 'anybody' had promised to attend. The Professor had said he could spare Azette to help; he was eagerly awaiting the turning of the tide, such was the force of the waves that they must shift hundreds of pebbles from the rocks, and who knew what interesting fossils would be uncovered.

The drawing-room was a riot of flowers, tulips of every hue predominated. Lady Monica, dressed in a powder blue suit, stood by the window; her two docile white poodles, who had been clipped from ribs to stern, stood by her side. She scanned Azette approvingly; she wore a neat cream blouse and a brown tailored skirt which, although of mini length, was not indecently short. Lady Monica could rely on her to help without obtruding herself.

Miss Marley entered the drawing-room dressed in glowing green. Spring had induced her to cast aside mauves and purples. Her lace jabot was secured by a ruby brooch, and ruby earrings swung from her ear lobes. She was followed by the immaculate Curtis who carried a brass tray and its stand.

'Thank you Curtis. If you will bring my biscuit tins and some plates,' Miss Marley twittered. 'Miss Renouf will help me make a pretty display.'

Azette heartily agreed with Miss

Marley when she vowed that nobody had seen such biscuits as those she had baked. Glace cherries had found their way on Raisen Rockies, Swiss Biscuits were topped with Walnuts, Oats were confused with Cornflakes, green colouring used to ice hearts and carraway seeds and coconut fought in Chocko Biscuits. Shortly before eleven Curtis wheeled in the trolley, and Mrs Curtis (wearing a spotless white overall) followed with a jug of steaming coffee and another of hot milk. She was to preside over the coffee cups whilst her husband answered the door. The gardener was already stationed outside the gates to superintend the parking of cars.

'I'm sure everyone will notice how fresh these chintz chair covers look Monica.' Miss Marley clasped her little hands proudly.

The clock chimed eleven and Lady Monica crossed the drawing-room with a flowing movement to greet the first guest with all the grace she could muster. She believed in giving value for money — not every woman could boast that she had drunk coffee with a real Lady.

Whilst this essentially feminine activity was taking place in the drawing-room, the Professor was impatiently watching the movements of the wild waves from the landing window. Directly after luncheon he called upon Azette to change her shoes, wrap up warmly and accompany him down to the beach. They were armed with baskets, hammers and chisels. The waves were tossing and grey as the wind rushed inland from the sea. Masses of seaweed, branches of trees, planks of wood and a decayed tree stump had been washed high on the shore. The whole aspect of the rocky ridge had changed; the turbulent sea had hurled the pebbles from it.

'Bless my soul.' The Professor dropped to his knees. 'The most flawless univalve. I must cut it out before the tide covers it with pebbles again.' He took his hammer and chisel from his basket, and suggested that Azette should occupy herself by looking for a further interesting find. She was already familiar with specimens of shell-fish, plants, teeth and bones of reptiles.

Whilst gulls shrieked wildly from secure crevices in the cliffs, Azette wandered along the shore keeping her eyes open for any fossils on the newly exposed rocks. She stopped and called to the Professor when she suspected she had found the fossil of a shell-fish on a slab of blue-grey rock. The Professor blessed his soul again. Azette offered to do her best to chip the shell-fish out. She was glad she had changed into the slacks she kept at the house to wear when walking in cold weather.

Soon Andrew came striding down the slipway and hailed the Professor. 'I came to give you a hand sir.'

'That's duced good of you Andrew,' the Professor shouted back. 'But haven't you things to attend to on the farm?'

'I've seen Posser and Green. Everything is under control.'

'Then perhaps you could lend Azette a hand. I don't want her to chip her fingers away. I've the blasted daylight, as well as the tide, to contend with; this univalve could keep me busy until dinner time.'

Azette surrendered her hammer to Andrew gladly; he positioned the chisel and when he struck it forcefully the Professor bellowed:

'A Gordon! A Gordon!'

'What made him say that?' asked Azette.

'It's the war cry of my clan.'

'Of course — the Gordons. I suppose you have your own tartan?'

'Yes.' Andrew was never very communicative.

'What is it like?' Azette asked trying to draw him out.

'A yellow stripe was introduced into the Black Watch pattern on the raising

113

of the Gordon Highlanders.'

Azette perched on a rock by Andrew's side, tied the mauve scarf Miss Marley had lent her more firmly round her neck, and listened interestedly whilst Andrew told her how the different tartans had come to be woven. When he altered his position to work round the other side of the fossil, Andrew changed his topic of conversation.

'I was interested to see you with Dennis on Saturday.'

'Why *interested*. Why not glad, curious or amused?'

'Because that is how I felt. Interested.'

'And did you think you understood how things were between us? You said you would when you met Dennis.'

'Yes, I understood your feelings for him.'

'Well?'

'You want the truth?'

'Of course.'

'I don't believe your feelings for Dennis go deeper than the love a sister

114

has for her brother. I think you and Dennis shared such a happy childhood, that when you meet now you unconsciously try to return to that childhood,' he summed up shrewdly.

'May be you are right.' Azette could not deny that. 'It used to be that way with my mother and Dennis's uncle when they were young; they had a wildly happy youth together, my mother often told me about it. Dennis is supposed to be very much like his Uncle Maurice.'

'Does he still live in Jersey?'

'No. He was killed in France shortly before the Armistice. Perhaps you have heard of him? He wrote detective books.'

'Ah, but of course, Maurice Maxted. My great-uncle had all his books, I enjoyed reading them when I stayed at Warren Farm for my school holidays. I suppose that sometimes when you went around with Dennis, you identified yourself with your mother and Maurice Maxted?'

'You have a knack of probing deeply Andrew.'

He paused in his work and glanced up at her. Her face above the soft folds of the mauve scarf looked very pensive. 'I'm sorry,' he offered. 'I should not have said that about your mother.'

'It doesn't matter.' Her hazel eyes softened forgivingly. 'But, since you seem so interested Andrew, I'll tell you something else. Uncle Maurice married my mother to save her being deported by the Germans. It was only a marriage of convenience.' Azette paused, then carried on because she had found it was so easy to confide in Andrew. 'But although Dennis is like Uncle Maurice, he is Uncle Adrian's son and, long before my mother married my father, she had quite a love affair with Uncle Adrian. I don't know how far it went, but sometimes I have seen how it was when they have avoided each other's eyes. So you see, Andrew, that something left over from that little romance could very well make itself felt between

Dennis and me one day.' She stood up uncertainly. 'There — I've told you things I should not have.'

Andrew laid down the hammer and faced her. 'I'll keep all your secrets, Azette, don't worry,' he assured her kindly.

She gave him a rather disturbed smile then crossed to tell the Professor that, before she returned to her typewriter, she would bring two flasks of tea down to the beach.

* * *

'Where are we heading, Dennis?' asked Azette on the following Sunday morning.

'Across these sands, and past that fall of rock,' responded Dennis strapping his easel more firmly over his shoulder.

'I don't mean that,' Azette walked unthinkingly through a pool of sea water. 'I mean what shall we be doing when the summer ends?' She turned up the wet hems of her jeans.

'In your case, I'd say it depends on how long it takes to finish the Professor's book.'

'Until September at least; he's re-writing some chapters.'

'After that you'll find a job in another office in St Helier I suppose.'

'I wonder. I feel I'm due for a change. What about you Dennis?'

'How can I say if we'll both live in Jersey again. We've spent over two years apart, and it seemed a very wrong state. But sometimes I feel we've only come together for a brief while.'

Gulls shrieked overhead. Azette looked up at the jutting grey cliffs; their faces were discoloured by rivulets of moisture, they reflected the sunlight until they stained the sand a dirty grey. Earlier that morning Dennis had stacked his painting gear in his sports car, and driven Azette to a coastal village from where they might walk to this place.

'I'm sure we could have found prettier spots Dennis.'

'At low tide that reef is a mosaic of small pools, their reflections are out of this world.'

'I don't see things through your eyes, even though we're so close Dennis. Compared to you, I might be colour blind.' Azette had faced up to the fact that she was not artistic by nature.

'You've been brought up to link colours with crops and harvests. To you Indigo means the grapes are ripe, to me it means transparent, mysterious depths in these pools. You associate Light Red with the Tomato Harvest, I regard it as being Life, and an indispensable good mixer.'

Azette moved away from the shadow of the cliff as, with a metallic click pieces of rusty tin slithered over the cliff edge. 'That's dangerous,' she gasped.

'There's a rubbish tip at the top,' exclaimed Dennis unperturbed. 'Every time the cliff crumbles, it brings down junk.'

Azette soon saw evidence of this; an oven, a child's push chair, old buckets and cycle frames littered the shore. When they reached the reef she spotted some twenty rusty drums in the rock pools.

'Won't those drums spoil your picture Dennis?'

'*I* can't see any drums.' Dennis took his bearings. 'This is where I stood last time.' He placed his paint-box on a slab of rock, and slid his easel off his shoulder. He had made a special container to carry wet canvases. 'I hope you brought something to read?'

'A Thomas Hardy; Jane says Dorset is the place to read his books. What time do you want lunch?'

'One will do. Be careful of the ale.'

Azette sat for two hours on the shingle with her back against an uncomfortable rock, she called Dennis every ten minutes from one o'clock to two o'clock. He joined her with a satisfied gleam in his strange flecked eyes; he quickly prized the stopper off a bottle of ale with his penknife.

'I'm damned hungry, what has Mrs

Preston put in my sandwiches?'

'Ham and lettuce, swop some for my cheese and tomato?'

'O.K. Remember the picnics we had in the old days?'

The tide turned whilst they reminisced about the carefree days when they had explored quaint bays in Jersey; they laughed at the many mishaps they had shared.

'I've been telling Mandy about Jersey,' Azette mentioned 'She needs a holiday, and Mum has invited her to stay on the farm.'

Dennis looked displeased. 'But I told Mandy I wanted to paint her portrait. Be a good girl, Azette, and arrange for her to sit for me in the evenings.'

Azette stood up and brushed crumbs from her jeans. She had told nobody but her mother and Andrew that Mandy was pregnant, and that had been for good reasons.

'I can't promise anything Dennis. Now I'm going for a walk further along the beach.'

Azette passed a battered clothes washer, and the rusty skeleton of a car; after this the beach was cleaner. Cliffs took on a creamy texture, grasses clawed at their face as if their life depended on the strength of their hold. Young trees clung to the edge of the cliff, they waved twisted arms in bravado, but every day, and every night, the sea surged to the cliff's base hoping to carry them off.

The contour of the cliff dropped to meet sand dunes. Azette spotted two children moving steadily up these. She thought they wore white T-shirts and grey shorts — a dark haired boy and a fair haired girl. She watched their progress until the silence was broken by screeching as gulls left nests in the cliff face. The children vanished, their places were taken by beating grey and white wings. Perhaps there had never been any children. Perhaps Azette had been living in the past, and had pictured herself climbing up La Pulente Dunes with Dennis fifteen years ago.

She turned back. The oncoming tide was filling the rock pools, and Dennis was putting his paints away. Azette praised his work. He had high-lighted green fronds of sea-lettuce, brown pod-weed, red pepper-dulse and purple laver. The blue sky was reflected in radiant pools, and bleached coral-weed, lichins and other sea-mats gave grey rocks a mystic quality.

They hastened to the fall of rock when they noticed the sea was creeping up to it. Azette choose to cross a patch of grey sand rather than climb over boulders; she sank up to her knees in quick-sand.

'Don't stand there like a loon,' Dennis cried urgently. 'Drag your feet out right away.' He held his easel out to her. 'Catch this.'

Azette curled her toes to get a grip on her canvas shoes, the practical side of her nature told her she would need them later; then she drew her right foot out of the sticky mess whilst catching hold of the extended easel. As she put her right foot forward, and set it down lightly, an evil force sucked her left foot downwards.

'I've lost my shoe,' she gasped.

'Damn your shoe. For God's sake hang on to the easel.'

Her right foot was sinking now, but her left was free. Dennis braced his feet against a small boulder to enable him to run his hands up the easel alternatively, and pull hard without losing ground. Azette came to him with a stumbling movement. Her jeans were covered in thick grey mud; when she stood by his side she avoided mentioning she had lost her other shoe.

She wondered, 'Why do things always — '

' — happen to us?' Dennis finished.

She looked aghast at her slimy jeans, then they both burst out laughing. But behind her laughter Azette felt uneasy, one day it might not be so easy to extract herself from such a mishap.

9

'It's in a shocking state isn't it?' said Andrew from behind Azette.

She was looking over the cob wall of Warren Farmhouse, she was looking for the mallard drake, or the duck who had been nesting in the ruined kitchen, but could not see them. How the weeds had grown since she had first seen the place. She found it hard to refrain from asking Andrew when he was going to do something about restoring the farmhouse. She frowned at the Rose Bay Willow Herb which abounded both inside and outside the house.

'That pink Willow Herb has taken possession Andrew.'

'It thrives on burnt ground,' he observed so bitterly that she was sorry she had been the cause of reminding him about the fire. But then he could hardly be expected to think of anything else whilst standing here. 'It was an attractive farmhouse,' he added broodingly.

'One day it could be that way again.' Azette wondered if Andrew lacked the heart to do something definite about the matter because of his rift with the glamour widow. 'Will the house be rebuilt on these foundations?'

'Yes,' he replied tersely. His expression changed as two brown haired children approached with Boy at their heels; they smiled broadly and their blue eyes danced. 'Half term already?' asked Andrew.

'Yes, Mr Gordon,' replied the boy who reminded Azette of the character 'William'. 'Please may Boy come for a walk with us?'

'Certainly; he will enjoy that.'

'We take care of him, and he takes care of us Mr Gordon,' the girl explained as she adjusted the red ribbons which held her hair in two bunches.

'That's the idea.' Andrew turned to

Azette. 'These are Posser's children, Dave and Sally.'

Azette gave them a friendly smile, and encouraged them to tell her how they went to the Primary in the village, and how the school 'bus picked them up from the road. Their Dorset accent was not as pronounced as their father's.

'Nice kids,' Andrew told Azette when they watched their progress down the lane. Sally's bunches swung as she skipped, and Dave picked up a stick shaped like a boomerang. 'They are something that all the money in the world can't buy.' (Azette wondered why Andrew's voice should be tinged with regret, it was not as though he was married.) 'Oh well,' he said. 'I want to take a look at the orchard. Coming?'

He took for granted she was, because he held the garden gate open for her. When they passed under the rose archway, clusters of crimson rambler roses trembled uncertainly, they needed more support. It was unlike Andrew to let things go, he worked tirelessly on his farm, and aimed to maintain the high standards of his great-uncle. He stepped into the orchard ahead of Azette. A wind had sprung up; the apple trees moved their blossom as if endeavouring to attract his attention. He looked up at their twisting branches.

'By God, but they must be pruned later. I should have seen to them properly before.' His voice sounded full of self reproach.

'Then why didn't you?' Azette wanted to say. She hated to see wastage on a farm. She bent to move her hand amongst the long thick grasses. 'Aren't you going to make use of this grass?' she felt bound to ask.

'So says the farmer's daughter,' smiled Andrew. 'And what do you suggest I do with it?'

'You could keep goats.'

'Goats!'

'Yes goats. My father has a beautiful flock of white goats. They are descendants of those bred on the farm belonging to Dennis's mother's family, the Le Bruns. Their milk is always in demand.'

Andrew listened, with both interest and amusement, as Azette described how, during the German Occupation of Jersey, her mother had hidden two R.A.F. men in her farm cellar. When the Germans were closing in on her, Pierre Le Brun had driven some of the goats across the island in a trap, the R.A.F. men had hidden under a seat. Azette's father had later crossed them to France in his motor boat.

'Your parents must be a great couple, I'd like to meet them one day, Azette.'

'They'd welcome you at any time. I've persuaded Mandy to spend a holiday with them soon.'

'That should cheer her up. Has she told you who the baby's father is yet?'

'No. But my mother is the sort of person she could confide in.' A picture came to Azette of Mandy seated in a small armchair by her sitting-room window embroidering a smock for herself; how young and vulnerable she looked. 'Mandy is so helpless in many ways, I often want to cry for her.'

'But you, being the practical person you are, try to do something to help her instead.' Andrew regarded Azette thoughtfully.

'She misses her own mother who died a few years ago. I thought a change of scenery would help her think clearer so that she would know what to do for the best.' Azette glanced at her watch. 'Oh, I've been talking too long.'

She bent her head to avoid knocking off apple blossom, but Andrew turned her to face him. She looked into his brown eyes warily; he had always disturbed her, and in some inexplicable way had often frightened her. Now he smoothed the flesh of her bare arms until she shivered, then he bent and kissed her full on the lips.

'You needed that,' he observed when he released her. 'I needed it too.' He twined his fingers tightly in hers as they crossed the orchard together.

'May must have missed her 'bus,' Lady Monica told her brother as he joined her and Azette in the hall the next day, after the luncheon gong had summoned them. 'I hope nothing has happened to her.'

'What could happen to May in Tollbury?' the Professor growled. 'The wolves don't chase a woman who is past mini skirts do they?'

Lady Monica was about to enter the dining-room when she was arrested by the pealing of the front door bell. 'No George,' she protested. 'Our front door has always been answered by a manservant.'

'That's so,' agreed the Professor. The bell pealed again — louder this time. 'I suppose Curtis is too busy clattering silver to hear that blasted row.'

Azette stood impassively with her back to the study door whilst this pathetic domestic scene ran its course. The library door opened and she heard

Andrew tell his dog to 'stay', then she heard his heavy footsteps crossing the hall. He halted by her side, and shot her an amused look as much as to say that he had summed up the situation. Nobody moved or spoke until Curtis walked past them with a measured tread.

'I thought you would never answer Curtis,' came Miss Marley's twittering voice. She crossed the Turkey carpet and came down the passage. 'I've had such a morning. I had a basket full of nice things, then I saw these oranges (but of course you can't see them because Curtis has taken my basket). I couldn't resist a dozen, but they rolled out of my basket, one after the other, in the road. I didn't know which orange to chase first; then a charming young man came to my rescue. He picked up every orange, but I didn't notice my 'bus move off until too late. Then this young man insisted on driving me home.'

'Thank God,' grunted the Professor. 'Otherwise you might be on a slow boat to China by now.'

'Oh but I shouldn't like to go to China George. Now I shan't be a moment washing my hands.' Miss Marley paused at the foot of the stairs to say, 'I forgot to tell you that I told Dennis he must stay to luncheon.'

'Dennis?' wondered Lady Monica.

'The young man who picked up my oranges turned out to be Azette's cousin. Curtis was to show him to the cloak-room.'

When Azette introduced her cousin to Lady Monica and the Professor, they regarded him favourably. They considered he looked remarkably hygienic for an artist, he was wearing a neat black corduroy suit, a white shirt and a wide emerald tie and his manners were beyond reproach. Mrs Curtis soon dished up the plaice and creamed potatoes, luckily there was plenty, and there was a substantial lemon sponge too. Miss Marley came tripping in to take her place at the head of the table; her cheeks were flushed prettily. She was aware that Michael was her brother's favourite young man, and Andrew was her sister's favourite. Now here, seated on her left hand, was somebody on whom she could bestow her favours; nobody could deny that Dennis had good breeding, and how she had enjoyed discussing the effects of brilliant colours with him on the drive up from Tollbury.

'I believe your father is a doctor, Dennis?' she mentioned so as to get this fact over to her snobbish sister right away.

'Yes,' responded Dennis easily. 'Doctoring is in my father's family; my grandfather was a doctor and my brother recently qualified. My mother comes from a farming family, as does my father's mother. She was a Renouf, the sister of Azette's father's father.' Dennis looked across the table at Azette, and his eyes seemed to gather her up possessively.

'But you decided that painting was your line?' observed the Professor affably.

'Yes. I also pebble pick to make ends meet.'

Lady Monica's throat was working as though she was endeavouring to swallow one of the pebbles. She looked round for somebody to share her horror; her eyes rested on Andrew.

'It is the recognized thing that our generation should undertake any type of work Lady Monica,' he explained as his eyes filled with amusement. 'You must remember how students have helped me during harvest times.'

'Andrew is right,' agreed the Professor. 'We must face up to the fact that although Warren House still keeps Father's traditions, young people of today have ways, and minds of their own.' He studied Dennis's lively face keenly. 'I believe you are to hold an exhibition?'

He fired questions at Dennis, and soon Lady Monica became so impressed with Dennis's answers, that she mentally listed wealthy friends whom she would ask to attend his exhibition. This was a conversation that held Miss Marley's interest sufficiently to prevent her day dreaming; she knew quite a bit about painting, her best friend had married a well known artist who lived in the West Country. The meal was a pleasant one, and afterwards Andrew led Dennis round to the old stable block, now used as garages, to give him a can of petrol. Azette waited at the gate where the trees, now in full leaf, cast dense shadows, Dennis was to drive her as far as the road where she planned to walk across a pasture and so circle back to the house.

'I liked the old people,' Dennis mentioned to her as he swung his sports car out of the gates. 'They belong to quite a different age from us, but I can tell you're happy working for the Professor.'

'I am. It's odd how things work out; if Miss Marley hadn't found your jersey, which proved you must be in the district, I'd not have taken this job on.'

'What would you have done then?'

'Stayed in Tollbury for a little longer, then given you up.'

'Glad you didn't, I like to have you around.'

It was sunny in the lane where wild roses and honeysuckle were in bud. Green had halted the tractor on a verge to enable Dennis to pass, he saluted him cheerfully. Azette felt warm and comfortable beside him; she wished she might accompany him to Dorchester where he was to bid for picture frames at an auction sale. His unexpected appearance at Warren House had transformed the solid routine of the Marleys' luncheon table to one of excitement; Azette had hardly spoken to Dennis, but he had been sitting opposite her, and he was her one link with her island home.

'Do you like that farming chap, Andrew?' he asked.

'Sort of — I don't find him easy to get to know, he seldom talks about himself to me, but I find him a very good listener.'

'Seemed a decent enough guy. Got a girl?'

'I don't think he has at present, but, if he had, I'm sure he'd not tell me about her.'

Dennis started to sing the Top of the Pops, and Azette joined in until his car screeched to a halt at the end of the lane. Azette jumped out regretfully, Dennis sung good-bye to the beat of his song, then he turned into the road. She opened the gate of one of Andrew's pastures, and closed it carefully after her. She wished she had not parted from Dennis before they had come to the end of the song.

10

'You'd better watch out,' warned Jane when Azette told her she would not be back on the late afternoon 'bus the next evening because she was going out with Andrew.

'Watch out for what Jane?'

Wrapped in towels, the girls were leaving the beach opposite Jane's flat; now the weather was warmer, they had taken to having a swim before going out for the evening.

'Watch out for Andrew of course. Didn't I tell you he has a way with women?'

'You also told me you suspected Andrew was the father of Mandy's child,' stated Azette sharply. 'If Andrew wants to seduce me, I guess he won't choose to have an audience of Dorset Horn Sheep. He is driving me up to the hills to see them.'

Jane shrugged her shoulders, then bent to remove a discarded bottle from the pebbles. 'I bet the person who left this here would have thought again had he realized that when it is smashed it could sever a kid's foot.' She dropped it into the rubbish bin at the top of the steps; she was mindful of the public's welfare, but Azette often wished this did not extend to inviting any 'drop out' who won her sympathy up to the flat. 'Come and watch the Water Polo with me this evening, Azette. They're a great crowd, we can go to a bar with them afterwards.'

Azette agreed to this. Dennis would be finishing a picture in his studio; now that the time for his exhibition was drawing near, she seldom saw him, but she felt that the time he gave to painting was worth while. She had written to tell her mother about Dennis's ambitions, her mother had replied that it was now up to Dennis to write to his father to explain how he had spent the past two years.

Azette had dismissed Jane's rather
spiteful remark concerning Andrew,
before he drove her down the leafy
lanes towards the hills the next evening.
She was intensely interested in all she
saw.

'Does any of this land belong to you
Andrew?' she asked after they had
crossed the main road.

'Only the potato and the barley
fields. The land ahead belongs to Mr
Gilmore, that's his farmhouse behind
the pines; my uncle bought the
downland from him years ago — that's
why the estate is split up.'

'I see. When are the shearing
machines coming?'

'On Monday. Do you want to come
and watch?'

'No. I watched shearing in Jersey
once; after the fleece was taken off in a
single piece, the sheep looked so
pathetically naked.'

'But I bet they were glad to be free of

their thick coats in the hot weather.' Andrew turned left where the lane narrowed. 'This leads to my shepherd's cottage — it's off the beaten track, a honeysuckle and roses sort of place, you'll like it.'

Mr Yaffle's cream washed cottage had a thatched roof and porch, the windows were small and the front door opened straight on to the lane; an elderly woman, wearing a print frock, came out to empty a large brown teapot into a ditch.

'Is this rural enough for you Azette?' Andrew asked as he pulled up on a verge.

'Oh yes.' She looked around her unhurriedly. 'I want to describe everything to my father when I write.'

Mrs Yaffle was pleased to see them, after Andrew had introduced her to Azette she said, 'We don't get many visitors other than our family up here Miss Renouf; there will be a pot of tea waiting for you when you come back from the pastures.'

There was an extensive view from the brow of the hill. Azette gazed down on to the scattered homesteads, and the large area of farming land, appreciatively until Andrew opened a gate and they entered a large pasture. It was then Azette saw the sheep.

'All the ewes are horned. They are remarkable,' she gasped. She left Andrew's side to inspect them closer; their brown rimmed eyes stood out from their white faces.

Andrew had joined Mr Yaffle who had been repairing a gap in the hedge. As the two men crossed the short grass together in Azette's direction they were discussing the use of electrified wire; she gathered the shepherd was slow to appreciate modern methods. He was a sturdy man nearing retiring age; he raised his felt hat with old fashioned courtesy to Azette, and she noticed his grey hair was as thick as the sheep's fleece.

'Mr Yaffle says he will be glad to talk sheep with you Azette,' Andrew told her indulgently. 'I'm going to take a look at the other hedges.'

Azette learnt from Mr Yaffle that the sheep would be branded after they were dipped; they had to be dipped once yearly by law, but were dipped at intervals throughout the year. When he was a young man, the sheep were sheared by hand, but, since the last war, more and more machines were taking over on the farms; he could not say whether it was a good thing, but, then, as his children said, he was slow to move with the times. Mr Gordon was very pleased with the condition of the flock's fleece. Did Azette know that lanolin was obtained from their wool?

Mr Yaffle's broad face grew increasingly alive as he told Azette about the pens he would build in the cold weather, he would pack hurdles with straw for walls and fix a thatch roof. His wife was not happy without a lamb to rear from a bottle in the lambing season. Azette took in all these facts until Andrew re-joined them. It was not until they were leaving the pasture did Azette notice that a black and white Welsh sheepdog was sitting by a patch of nettles regarding the flock grimly; he did not appear to be a friendly dog and Azette understood why Andrew avoided taking Boy with him when he drove to the downland.

The interior of Mr Yaffle's cottage was, in contrast to the sheepdog's surly manner, very friendly. A savoury smell came from the kitchen range, a kettle boiled and coke glowed. Azette was invited to sit beside Andrew on the wooden settle, it was all very cosy if rather too warm. Mrs Yaffle handed round tea and sultana cake, then she spoke of their five children, and, as each name left her lips, her husband took a photograph from the dresser to display it proudly. This action was repeated when it became the turn of the numerous grandchildren. After the last photograph had been replaced on the dresser, Mrs Yaffle said she must feed her bees. Azette watched as the woman removed a piece of butter muslin from the top of a large Kilner jar which stood on the window sill. During the display of photographs, Azette had had half an eye on the extraordinary little sponge like bees which were moving up and down in the liquid in the jar. Now Mrs Yaffle dropped a teaspoonful of sugar into this.

'Those bees are even more unusual than the horned sheep,' cried Azette greatly fascinated by them.

Andrew chuckled. 'You didn't think they were real bees did you Azette? Special yeast at the bottom of that jar collects into those bee like lumps which rise up to the surface.'

'But what makes them sink again?'

'The gas they hold is dispersed when they reach the surface.'

Azette met Andrew's amused eyes and felt completely at home with him. She could feel the heat of his body as they shared the settle; the warm kitchen made her drowsy and, as she watched the bees go up and down, she was

146

blissfully content.

Later Mr Yaffle reached for his tobacco jar, and Mrs Yaffle asked Azette if she would like to see round the cottage. The evening sun flooded the parlour with a soft pinky glow, everything was very tidy, but it was different on Sundays explained Mrs Yaffle when her children and grandchildren drove up the hill. After Azette had admired the old bread oven flanking the stone fireplace, and the tapestry suite, she followed her hostess up the twisting staircase. She was shown the modern bathroom which was originally the box room, and was ushered into three small bedrooms in turn.

'What a pity Mr Gordon has been so unlucky with women,' Mrs Yaffle pronounced unexpectedly as she smoothed her patchwork bedspread. She eyed Azette curiously. 'There is nothing like a good marriage.' Azette maintained a blank expression but Mrs Yaffle ploughed on. 'That widow lady was too old for him. She was very attractive, but it was only summer madness. He needed her to help him recover from that terrible happening.'

The old woman paused as they heard men's voices calling them. So the glamour widow had only been 'summer madness' thought Azette as she descended the twisting stairs. But what was the terrible happening that Andrew needed to recover from? Why did he avoid discussing his private life? After they had said good-bye to the shepherd and his wife, they drove through the cooling air without talking until Andrew parked the car outside a brightly painted inn called *The Shearers Arms*.

'Unfortunately this is the nearest inn to Warren House, Azette. It's a very old building, but has been modernised inside.'

They sat on stools at the bar counter, drank Dry Martinis and ate a well cooked basket meal of scampi and chips.

'You're an easy girl to take out Azette; I feel at home with you.

Admittedly the fact that you're so attractive makes being with you doubly enjoyable.' Andrew looked hard at Azette's shapely legs which were twined round the metal legs of the stool. 'How's Dennis getting along with his painting?'

'He's frantically busy so I don't see much of him.' Azette described his work, then blurted out, 'Sometimes Dennis doesn't feel like my cousin any more.'

'Then it might be better if you didn't tag along together often.'

'Why?'

'You might be hurt if you hoped for too much.'

'I don't understand you.' She gave him a puzzled look.

'I was thinking that one day you might decide your relationship with Dennis had ceased to resemble the relationship your mother had with Dennis's Uncle Maurice. You might decide it had become like the relationship she had had with his father.'

'And if it did?' she challenged him.

'You're too nice a person to have an unhappy love affair.'

She had nothing to say to that; it was time for Andrew to speak about himself instead.

'How many are there in your family Andrew?'

'My parents and my brother Hugh. He is two years older than I am; he is married to an exceptionally nice girl called Barbara, they have a cute kid called Christabel and a baby son. They live half a mile from the farmhouse in two cottages which have been thrown into one. Hugh has taken over the dairy herd, and my father concentrates on free-range poultry now. My mother was a school-mistress, she's a very patient sort of person, clever too. Once I took them for granted. Now I realize what marvellous parents they've been to us. Come and meet them, Azette, next time I go down to Cornwall for a weekend — after the summer harvests that will have to be.'

Azette considered his suggestion

slowly; this was the first time Andrew had spoken of his family, now he had invited her to stay with them. 'Ask me again nearer the time, Andrew.' She eyed him thoughtfully. 'How did you feel when you left your home to take over Warren Farm?'

'At first I felt good because I had the chance to prove what I could do by myself on a farm. Later, when I thought I'd done that, I'd feel lonely at times, there were gaps that could not be filled. I — ' He broke off and paused for so long that Azette wondered if he would continue. 'The Professor and his sisters saw how it was with me, I told them — told them things. They were very understanding, I owe a great deal to them. There are certain things I can't speak of often.' He broke off abruptly.

Mrs Yaffle had said that Andrew had needed the widow to help him recover from 'that terrible happening'. Now he wanted to run away from it because he suggested hurriedly:

'Let's go for a drive Azette.'

★ ★ ★

Azette enjoyed the drive through Thomas Hardy's country so much that, when she arrived back at the flat, all she wanted to do was to go to bed and think about Hardy's novels. But Jane was entertaining two of her dropout friends; Azette did not understand why she mixed with such strange young men when she had Michael. She sat in an armchair sewing buttons on a greasy denim jacket belonging to a savage looking lout who lay back in the armchair opposite her. He was called Scrumpy Joe, and his conversation was restricted to grunts. His companion wore a dusty wine velvet suit; he sat cross legged on the floor and swayed backwards and forwards.

'It's part of Uriah's religion to sit that way,' Jane explained.

Uriah took one look at Azette and declared in a thin reedy voice, 'I love you.'

'It's part of his religion to love

152

everybody,' Jane put in hastily.

Uriah narrowed his eyes and studied Azette soulfully. 'Your aura is green.'

Jane giggled, snapped off a thread and threw the denim jacket at Scrumpy Joe. 'Oh, Dennis phoned, Azette. His exhibition is off because there's trouble over the hiring of the hall. Dennis will come round in the morning to tell you all about it.'

Azette's spirits sank. Her enjoyable drive was forgotten; now she would go to bed worrying over her cousin's troubles.

11

Dennis was inconsolable when he called at the flat the following morning — Saturday. Jane switched off the vacuum-cleaner, and Azette left the table she was polishing to ask:

'What has gone wrong Dennis? I thought it had been arranged that you could hire the hall.'

'It was almost in the bag, but then this chap Ludlow protested.'

'Why?'

'He owns a large art shop in Denethorpe, he resents competition.'

'But you were only going to hire the hall for a few weeks,' said Jane.

'Those weeks are part of the high season.' Dennis bent to re-tie the laces of his canvas shoes. 'Better buy a new pair of rope-soles if I'm going to pebble-pick for the rest of my life,' he frowned moodily.

'Don't be silly.' Azette protested sharply. 'You can't give up painting. Something must be done.'

'What? Tell me what?'

'Have some coffee Dennis?' was the only suggestion Jane could make.

'No thanks. I'm on my way to help Billy.'

'Shall I see you tomorrow?' Azette asked. 'We could go swimming Dennis.'

'I'm not keen. I'd rather start Mandy's portrait.' Dennis noticed the look Jane gave Azette, and questioned irritably, 'What's wrong with that?'

Jane told him. 'Mandy flew to Jersey yesterday morning to stay with Azette's mother. Michael drove her to the airport.'

Dennis's face darkened, his eyes filled with despair as he ran his fingers through his hair nervously.

'Why on the hell did you have to cook that up without telling me? Now my exhibition has fallen through, the only thing I want to do is to paint Mandy, but — no, I can't even do that thanks to you girls. God knows why you've done all you can to keep me from seeing Mandy again.'

He threw the hall door open and slammed it after him. It hurt Azette that he had looked to Mandy to console him instead of to her.

* * *

'You'll not go near the wreck of the *Emma* will you George?' begged Miss Marley as he threw the drawing-room windows open prior to leaving Warren House with Michael for a fishing trip on Monday afternoon.

'I'll not contemplate suicide until my book is published,' the Professor growled as Michael helped him into his old windcheater.

'You two men will wear your life jackets?' Miss Marley insisted.

'You'll have us wearing bibs next, May. But anything to save you worrying.' The Professor turned to Azette. 'Ah you have my gloves; my hands get deuced cold lately.'

Azette and Miss Marley watched the Professor cross the garden with Michael who had been invited to round off the afternoon by staying to dinner. Azette had been invited too, and Jane was to catch the 'bus up after work. The sea was calm, and there was a shoal of mackerel in the bay.

'Curtis will bring tea soon Azette. You will keep me company won't you?' Miss Marley twittered. 'My sister won't be back until ten o'clock; that's very late.' As Azette moved two chairs to a sunny spot by the window, Miss Marley asked, 'Is your cousin ready for his exhibition?'

'It has been cancelled Miss Marley.' Azette explained the situation to the old lady, but doubted if she took everything in because she had a faraway air.

But she said, 'I thought you looked troubled during luncheon my dear. The other day Monica drove me to the Tollhouse to see Dennis's work. His colours! They are glorious. He's a most gifted young man.'

Miss Marley was engrossed in her crochet when Azette left her to return to her typewriter. She was still typing when she saw Jane coming down the drive, she wore a short white jacket and a green summer frock, and had caught her red hair up as she did when visiting her family. She was a different Jane from the one who knocked around with lay-abouts and drop-outs. By the time Azette had covered her typewriter, and changed her blouse and skirt for an ice blue frock, a mist was creeping stealthily over the ivy and through the gorse. Jane was prowling restlessly round the drawing-room.

'Is there anything worth seeing on television?' she asked her aunt.

Miss Marley took up the *Radio Times*. 'There's this film about a shipwrecked man on a raft — '

'Would you mind if Azette and I went for a short walk, Aunty, whilst you watch the film?'

'No, you go dear. You can give these

cake crumbs to my robin.' Miss Marley fumbled for a bag stuffed behind the cushion of her Sheraton chair.

The girls took the track through the woods, and paused to scatter crumbs under a young beech; a robin hopped across decaying leaves. He put his head on one side to listen before pecking at his supper.

'We'll be able to see Uncle's boat from this bank,' Jane told Azette.

'Where is the wreck of the *Emma*?' Azette asked after they had pushed their way between gorse and briers.

'Round that point, there's nothing to see. It happened a long time ago, a yacht was caught on a reef.'

'Surely it's too far for your uncle to go?'

'Don't forget he has an outboard motor.'

'But there must be plenty of mackerel close to Warren Beach.'

'Men always want to go a little further when in a boat.' Jane moved a branch of a pine aside. 'Like when there're out with a girl.' She pointed out to sea. 'There's Uncle's boat; I wish they wouldn't go out so far. That headland will soon be obscured.'

A breeze had wafted through the woods; it drove the mist from the west, and screened the Professor's boat.

'Let's go back to the house,' suggested Azette. 'We can't do any good standing here worrying.'

The girls' shoes sank into rotting vegetation as they hastened back to the track. Jane told Azette the story of the *Emma*; the telling of it fitted in with her depressive mood.

'The yacht's owner had persuaded a young wife to run away with him; according to the crew who managed to swim ashore, they sailed from Falmouth and all went smoothly until the woman regretted leaving her young children. Her lover refused to turn back; when they reached the Dorset coast, there was a terrible storm, they were forced to seek shelter inshore. The lovers were drowned on the reef. Fishermen said they heard the woman crying for her children when they sailed close to the wreck. Those who passed over it swore it was haunted because they lost control of their steering. But Michael says cross currents over the reef forced the fishermen to lose control of their boats.'

'How does he account for the poor woman's cries?'

'He says that when the wind blows through a gap in the rocks it sounds like a woman wailing.' Jane jumped down on to the track thankfully.

A mist had closed in on Warren House. The girls found Miss Marley asleep in front of the television. Outside ghostly maidens laid transparent hands on the windows.

'It will be kinder if you don't turn the T.V. off Jane,' Azette suggested softly. 'It will wake your aunt, then she'll start worrying.'

'O.K. Let's go and ask Andrew what he thinks we ought to do about the boat.'

Andrew was seated at a large walnut

table which stood in the centre of the library; it was littered with accounts and other papers. His dog was beside him with his head resting on his front paws. They appeared to be isolated from the rest of that lofty room where books lined the walls, and show-cases of small stuffed animals stood alongside hide armchairs.

'Don't get up Andrew,' Jane said in a sugar sweet tone. 'I can see you're busy.' She avoided clods of mud which had fallen from Andrew's boots, and stepped closer to the table. 'Uncle went fishing with Michael this afternoon; now they're lost out there in the mist. What ought we to do?' She frowned worriedly.

'Firstly stop worrying, Jane; neither your uncle or Michael would dream of moving on unless they could see where they were going. But I will have a word with the coastguard.'

Andrew felt for the telephone, Azette moved some bills aside and passed him the receiver. When he had spoken to the coastguard, he smiled reassuringly.

'The coastguard says not to worry; the mist is already thinning. The boat should be in shortly Jane, we'll all go down to meet it eh? Meanwhile perhaps you'd better tell Mrs Curtis to hold dinner,' he suggested.

'I'll do that Andrew.' Jane looked happier now. 'Coming Azette?'

'Azette hasn't been in the library before, she wants to take a look at the show-cases,' Andrew stated firmly.

Azette studied the fox, the grey squirrels, the stoats, the weasels, the badgers and the rabbits.

'I saw a badger in Warren Woods one afternoon Andrew.'

'That's unusual, they're nocturnal creatures.'

'I'm always on the lookout for a deer.'

'The Fallow Deer is fine in its natural setting, but can be very destructive. One would make short work of Lady Monica's garden. I found some shed antlers in the woods last winter, so watch out.'

'But you warned me not to go near the jungle, there must be places which are out of this world?'

'There is such a place.' Andrew did not elucidate but studied Azette appreciatively. 'That pale blue suits you.'

'Oh thanks.' Azette glanced at the bay window. 'The mist is thinning, I'd better see if Miss Marley is still asleep.'

'I suppose you'd better, but it's been nice to have you here with me.'

The television blared in the drawing-room, Miss Marley slept blissfully. Azette turned to the french windows and watched the ghostly maidens move across the lawn with their white robes and gossamer hair streaming out behind them. They vanished into a shrubbery. Then Jane hastened into the room.

'I spotted the boat from the landing window, it's heading inshore, get your coat Azette.' As the girls crossed the garden, Jane sighed, 'I wish I wasn't so bitchy to Michael.'

'I expect he does too.' Azette disliked

the way Jane would pick Michael up, and set him down to suit her convenience.

Andrew and Curtis joined the two girls by the water's edge as the boat came in. When it scraped on the pebbles, the Professor growled:

'Why the reception committee?' He grudgingly allowed Andrew to help him ashore, he looked cold. 'What the devil is in that flask?' he demanded of Curtis.

'Coffee, sir.'

'And — ?'

Curtis whispered in his ear, and unscrewed the stopper of the flask as he led his master homewards. Jane took up the basket of mackerel, grasped Michael's arm possessively, and marched him up the lane.

Azette turned to Andrew who was clearing some weed from the bottom of the boat. 'That's the best thing about being part of a family,' she remarked thoughtfully. 'You're never alone when there's trouble.'

'Homesick?' asked Andrew kindly.

'I have my moments; it's nice to know that Mandy is staying with my family; she'll be able to tell me all their news when she returns. I'm sure her holiday will help her to think clearer, I hope she will contact the father of her baby when she comes back.'

'Yes, she ought to give him the chance to help her; she won't find it too easy to bring up a baby alone.' Andrew passed Azette the Professor's life jacket. 'If you can hang this up, I can manage the boat.'

Azette hung up the life jacket on a hook in the corner of the hut, then turned and watched Andrew as he passed his hand over the curve of the boat. His hands were strong and capable, she knew they could be gentle too. During the past few weeks she had decided he was a very likeable person, she was not in love with him but now, perhaps because she needed comforting, she wanted to be close to him.

'Boat building must be an interesting craft,' he observed.

Andrew was still examining the construction of the boat when a sea breeze slammed the doors of the hut, and Azette moved uneasily; although she wanted to be close to Andrew, at the same time she feared to be. His eyes were holding hers now, it was like the time she had first met him in the café scullery. She was afraid because she did not know what was behind his searching look. Was he comparing her with somebody else? The glamour widow perhaps. When he made no move she wondered if he was looking at her, or through her; could he be re-living that 'terrible happening' that Mrs Yaffle had spoken of?

She strove to free him by reminding him, 'We must not be late for dinner Andrew.'

'Y — es, of course,' he responded slowly. 'Where did the Professor leave the key?'

'It's in the lock.'

He pushed the doors open, and she stepped out on to the pebbles after him.

They reached Warren House in time to hear Curtis sound the gong. Miss Marley had brushed her hair and changed into a shapeless evening gown.

'Ah there you are Azette. I have splendid news. You will remember I told you that my old friend is married to Roy Halt the artist. Well they live in Denethorpe, so I telephoned Roy and told him about Dennis's upset. Roy is a councillor and said he will put an end to Mr Ludlow's pranks. Dennis can certainly have the use of the hall as planned, Roy wants him to telephone him as soon as possible.'

Azette thought Miss Marley was a wonder, and told her so.

'Did you think I was asleep all the time you girls were wandering about in that mist?' Miss Marley's cheeks flushed happily. 'I found Dennis's jersey in the woods, so it is right I should be the one to help him now.'

12

Azette was thinking of her cousin when she took a walk in the woods after her lunch; due to the efforts of Miss Marley's artist friend, Roy Halt, the hall had definitely been allocated to Dennis. His black mood had left him, and he had thrown himself enthusiastically into the final preparations for the hanging of his oils. He had thanked Miss Marley by presenting her with a painting of a colourful bowl of tulips which she had much admired. Now Azette half expected to see Miss Marley pop out unexpectedly from a thicket. Eggs had been hatched, this was an interesting time for bird watchers; but this afternoon the woods were silent until Azette heard distant voices.

She was surprised to see a group of people cross the track where it met Faraway Lane. They were middle aged, and surely too old to walk through the miles of jungle which Andrew had warned Azette lay ahead. They carried walking sticks and knapsacks, and moved purposefully. Azette was most curious to see where they were heading. She swung her legs over the fallen elm, sought the cover of young silver birch and followed them silently. A grey squirrel ran out from behind a blackberry bush, she had startled it; it scuttled ahead holding its tail comically. To Azette's astonishment, the party appeared to be stalking it; they left Faraway Lane and, with one accord, pushed through the bracken. Both men and women wore jerseys, slacks and stout shoes and, as they formed a single file to take an almost imperceptible pathway, they appeared to be on a pilgrimage.

Their way was blocked by an uprooted oak; a steep rise in the ground supported this ancient tree's top branches. The ivy swarming over it had doubtless caused its ultimate destruction; the dry rottenness of its white-grey trunk indicated it could have rested there for at least thirty years. Azette spotted the tip of the squirrel's tail as it ran under the curtain of gleaming ivy; it was followed by the pilgrims who plunged into the greenery and crawled under the oak one after another.

'Wherever can they be going?' Azette muttered to herself.

She *had* to know, but it was time for her to return to work; she had left for her walk later than usual, Lady Monica had wanted to show her round her rose garden. One day, when she left the house earlier, she would find out where the mysterious pathway led, then she might know why these elderly people thought it worth while worming their way under that tree trunk in such an undignified manner. Storm clouds gathered that night and, for the remainder of the week Azette was prevented from walking in the woods by intermittent rain. Even so she constantly wondered what lay on the other side of that curtain of ivy.

At Warren House everyone was engrossed in his, or her, own affairs. Lady Monica held another charity coffee morning, Miss Marley was finishing some crochet work for a Church Fête, the Professor was discussing with Michael which of the photographs of his fossils would best illustrate his book, and, in between rain showers, Andrew was supervising the lifting of early potatoes. The soil was dry, it mopped the rain up like a sponge so that the potato field never became unworkable. Mandy sent happy postcards from Jersey, and Jane had made friends with some newcomers to Tollbury. They lived rough, sleeping in shelters, camping on the foreshore or even sneaking into empty property at night; they had no intention of working, they loafed on the beaches by day, drank 'Scrumpy' in the bars in the evenings and lived off the dole. Azette could find nothing in common with them, but Jane insisted they were great fun.

Azette was sure the hot sunshine on

Sunday must have dried the muddy patches in the woods, and, directly after luncheon on Monday, she hurried down the grassy track to Faraway Lane; from here she crossed the stretch of bracken and moved aside the curtain of ivy to enable her to crawl under the uprooted oak.

Then she was standing upright in a small spinny hemmed in by thickets. She smoothed her hair, and pulled her cotton frock into place before she took the path that ran towards the sea which gleamed beyond some pines. The air became progressively warmer, and smelt sweetly of wild thyme. Azette paused beside a palm tree; it was so like the one in her farm garden in Jersey. She gave its unusual bark a friendly slap before continuing down the path which ran alongside a brook. It babbled past exotic wild flowers to the sea. Higher up were masses of beautiful shrubs which attracted white butterflies.

Presently Azette came to a mere slip of a cove; green verges sloped gently down to a sandy beach across which the waves advanced. They were of little consequence, but they soughed continuously. Azette was entranced, she stood quite still on the soft sand whilst slowly absorbing the wonder of it all. When at length she turned her back on the sea, she saw Andrew standing on the verge above her. 'This must be yours,' he said without preamble. He threw the belt from her frock down to her; she was too astonished to catch it, and it fell at her feet. 'Who gave you permission to come down here?' he asked harshly.

'Did I need permission? One day last week I saw a party of hikers going down Faraway Lane, I saw them plunge into that curtain of ivy and crawl under the tree, I thought it odd as they were elderly so could not be too active.'

'They are active enough to be professional botanists,' Andrew responded scathingly. 'And they will be coming here every year with my permission.'

'Oh.' Azette picked up her belt then,

and tied it round her slim waist. 'Why do they need your permission Andrew?'

'Because Faraway Cove, and the woodland flanking Faraway Lane, happens to be my property. Some of the wild flowers growing here are very rare; those botanists were friends of my uncle's. Only they know where to find the rare orchid which grows in this valley, if its whereabouts is known it could become extinct in these parts.'

Andrew folded his arms, and stood with legs astride looking down at Azette challengingly as if ready to crush any comment she might make. She had never seen him looking so grimy, his hair was dusty and his face was streaked with dirt. He had not been at the luncheon table; the Professor had mentioned that haymaking had commenced, and Andrew had been up since dawn. Understandably he was tired, irritable and very warm.

'I'm very sorry I came here Andrew.'

He sprang from the verge to land by

her side. 'I count on being able to swim stark here.'

'Then I promise I'll never tell anyone about this cove.'

'Good. Its whereabouts would soon get around if you did.' He watched as she crossed to the rocks which formed steps to the verge. Then he was after her. 'This is the sort of place where I could easily make love to you.' He pulled her to him, and kissed her forcefully whilst passing his hand over her breasts.

'But you are not going to make love to me, Andrew,' she said despite the fact that the very earthliness of his appearance made him more disturbing; this afternoon he was so much a part of the soil. She fingered a tear in his shirt, under it his flesh was tanned and exciting. She told him, with a calmness she did not feel, 'You had better cool off in the sea.'

'You are right,' he agreed. 'You're too nice a girl to have casual sex. I'm sorry.'

She gave him a forgiving smile, and

was soon walking up the path where the brook babbled and glinted in the sunshine; she sensed she would never know where the rare orchid grew.

★ ★ ★

The sun beat down on Warren farm land for the rest of that week. In the hay field, it glinted on the long cutter-bar of the mower which stretched out to one side of the tractor. For two days swathes of the hay lay in long neat rows; then a side-delivery rake turned them so that the underside could also be dried by the sun. Afterwards it was the turn of the Pick-up baler which gathered the hay, packed it into bales and bound them with wire ready to be stored in the Dutch barn. Sometimes Azette would watch Andrew and Green at work in the field; the scent of the hay was sweet, but she doubted if the men had the time to appreciate it.

The next week Andrew took some ewes to the sheep fair to be auctioned.

Soon he would be thinking of the grain harvest, and arranging for the Combine Harvester to come.

'If it wasn't for my Exhibition, I would paint that field next week Azette,' Dennis told her when he met her at the 'bus stop on her way home from work one evening. He had left his car, and was leaning over the gateway of Andrew's corn field. 'Imagine the play of sun and shade on young corn,' he sighed.

Azette could only guess at the golds, and creamy glints, which Dennis would have mixed on his palette to paint the cornfield before the giant machine took over, and robbed the scene of much of its beauty. Since she had met up with her cousin again, she had learnt that he frequently lived in a place where, because of her practical outlook, she could not enter. She would be left dithering outside his colourful artistic world where he raved about half-tones, tints and colour blending. She had not yet learnt the difference between lemon yellow, cadmium yellow and yellow ochre, and avoided getting involved in discussing things she did not understand with Dennis.

This evening he was to drive her to the exhibition hall so that she might give him a hand with the final hanging of his paintings. He talked about them ceaselessly as they drove through the sunny countryside, and the outskirts of Denethorpe.

The evening sun was streaming through the windows of the exhibition hall when Dennis unlocked the double doors, and threw them open dramatically. Azette uttered an exclamation of admiration, she had seen all Dennis's work before and sensed it was excellent although knowing little about art; but now his paintings were hanging in good light, and a pleasing setting, they appeared even more wonderful to her. She felt enormously proud of her cousin: surely his exhibition could not fail to be a success.

'Now don't stand there gaping

Azette. I need help with those pictures over there.' Dennis was climbing a step-ladder. 'All you have to do is to pass them up to me in their order, then step back to tell me if I have hung them straight, that'll save — '

' — bags of time,' she finished as she took off her cardigan and threw it over a chair.

Azette was very happy helping Dennis; every time a picture was hung she felt he was one step nearer to returning home to his parents in Jersey. Time passed, and everything went smoothly until Dennis was obliged to move the step-ladder to the other side of the room; he swung it round so exuberantly that it crashed straight through a window. He swore loudly.

'Now don't tell me that we always run into trouble when we're together Azette, or I'll crown you.'

'I won't.' Azette opened a door hopefully; it led to a small passage off which she discovered a broom cupboard. Whilst she swept up broken glass she urged, 'I noticed a builder's yard when you parked your car, Dennis, you'd better hurry and see if a glazier can come early in the morning. Your exhibition will be ruined if brown paper is flapping over that broken pane.'

Dennis was out of the double doors in a flash, and soon returned with the news that a glazier would be along to take measurements, and would glaze the next day.

'Now, let's get cracking again Azette. We'll start on that lot now. I haven't hung the parrot yet.' He placed the ladder to his satisfaction and grinned cheerfully. 'Not to worry, might have put this ladder through one of my masterpieces instead.' He climbed the ladder excitedly.

But the incident of the broken window-pane left Azette feeling uneasy. Did a jinx control their movements when they were together? She wanted Dennis's exhibition to be a success more than anything in the world. If it was, she was sure that he had a future

181

as a brilliant artist.

'What did you think of the printing of my hand-bills?' he called down to her.

'Oh, great.'

The glazier came then to measure the window frame. When he left the sun was going down and Dennis had hung his last picture. He switched on all the lights, and Azette could see his strange flecked eyes glittering with pride.

'Everything is ready now for the opening on Monday.' He paced round the room optimistically. 'Nothing can go wrong now.' He switched the lights out with a gratified sigh. 'Thanks for your help, my love. I'll take you out somewhere special on Sunday for a treat.'

13

'I shall give you the time of your life this morning Azette,' Dennis predicted cheerfully when she joined him on the harbour the next Sunday. 'You look fantastic in those white shorts, the very thing for this speed boat.'

'Whose is it?'

'A chap lent it to me. We'll be back in time for drinks and sandwiches at the *Sailors' Inn.*'

Azette's eyes lit up; the weather was perfect for boating of any description. The few vessels still in the harbour rocked gently, their shadows shimmered in the turquoise water as if impatient to be off out of the harbour. Azette hurried down a flight of stone steps after Dennis, and stepped into a speed boat which (he assured her) was seaworthy, even if in need of a lick of paint. Dennis told his cousin where to sit, then cast off, he picked his way carefully between sailing craft until they were out of the harbour. Then he turned westwards and gathered up speed; the bow of the *Sweet Sue* was well out of the water, and the stern zoomed through the sea like a rocket. Azette clutched her seat to prevent herself being thrown overboard; the air whipped her hair back and nearly took her breath away.

They shot past the pebble beach below Warren House which looked serene and secure behind the wattle fencing. Then Azette sighted the beautiful little Faraway Cove, and the green valley behind it. She wondered if Andrew would be swimming from it today; he was a man who could be content with his own company although he frequently spent Sunday with friends from the Speed Boat Club.

'Thought you'd like to see the beach where we pebble pick,' Dennis cried as he reduced speed. He indicated a cove which was larger than the rest. 'There are enough pebbles to last Billy a life time.'

'I can see that. But how did you manage to climb up to the woods when you left your jersey on the fallen elm?'

'Easy. I took those jutting pieces of cliff one at a time as though they were stepping stones. Hold on,' Dennis yelled happily.

The *Sweet Sue* gathered speed, and raced on past isolated coves until they reached the extremity of Tollbury Bay, then Dennis lost all control of the steering wheel. The engine stalled and the boat drifted aimlessly on the blue sea.

Dennis cursed in astonishment. 'The works have packed up!'

Azette sat very still. She was not surprised, something unfortunate was bound to happen when she was out with Dennis. She remembered her mother's description of how, when she was out boating with Dennis's Uncle Maurice, they had been thrown out of the rowing boat and nearly drowned.

'A current must have carried us over this reef Azette. I felt a tug on the boat as though it was being pulled by an invisible rope.'

Azette paled. 'Haven't you heard about the Wreck of the *Emma*?' she asked. 'We're over it now.'

'You don't believe in such superstitious stuff do you?' Dennis scoffed. He was fumbling with a switch. 'That's the worst of these old engines. Anything can happen.'

'It has, hasn't it?' uttered Azette with icy calm. 'They say the wreck is haunted.'

'Rubbish.'

'They say the young wife who drowned can be heard crying for her children.'

'That's the gulls shrieking you clot.'

'Why are you making the boat circle?' Azette asked sharply.

'I'm not. The bloody steering won't respond.'

'Perhaps it is because — '

' — the wreck was cursed,' Dennis

finished. 'Obviously it's a freak current.' He studied the coast line. There were miles of soaring cliffs fringed with grey and blue pebbles and topped with a green jungle. 'The tide is coming in, we'll be carried ashore if — '

' — we're lucky. There must be submerged rocks as well as the wreck, best get ready to swim for it Dennis.'

Presently, when the boat's prow was pointing to the shore, it suddenly gave up circling and lazy breakers carried it slowly to the beach.

'Thank God,' Dennis sighed. 'I don't think this boat's insured.'

They dragged the *Sweet Sue* high on the foreshore to a spot where Dennis told Azette the sea could not reach it. Billy would help him pick it up at dawn the next day when they went pebble picking.

'But you're opening your exhibition then Dennis.'

'Of course. Force of habit. I'll make it worth while if Frank helps Billy.'

'I expect the friend who lent you the

Sweet Sue will raise the alarm?'

'He's gone on holiday. Well, I'd better look for the safest place to climb to the top. You can watch for a passing boat.'

Azette stood on the pebbles whilst the tide hissed towards her, it laid a mass of seaweed at her feet, red fern like pieces, a piece of sponge and a dead star-fish. Some cormorants alighted nearby, but when the waves frothed up to them, they took off again and their cries echoed across the beach; they could resemble the sad cries of a woman. When Azette sighted a fishing boat, she waved repeatedly, but the fishermen could not have seen her.

Soon Dennis trudged back over the uncomfortable pebbles, he pointed to the face of the cliff. 'There's something of a path up there. Are you game Azette?'

'If you think it's better than being stuck here until somebody rescues us?'

'I don't think anybody will pass close enough to see us. They keep away because of that yarn about the haunted wreck.' Dennis assured his cousin optimistically. 'Once we climb this cliff, our troubles will be over.'

It was a hazardous climb up the cliff face; Azette would not have attempted it had she not climbed so many cliffs in Jersey with Dennis. She went slowly and calmly; she had always gone first because Dennis could then time his movements to fit in with hers, and, should she waver, he would be ready with cheerful advice. Her knees and hands were cut and bleeding when she reached the top; she stepped straight into a dense jungle of greenery, elderberries and ivy. In her breathless state, she fancied it snarled at her.

Shafts of sunlight forced their way between the leaves and revealed secret places under trees; there were strange rustlings in branches overhead and unaccountable movements in the undergrowth. Shrubberies of bamboos whispered, silver birch shook their elegant branches and pines muttered amongst themselves. Soon the cousins were engulfed in a vast sea of greenery so powerful that Azette felt she could have drowned in it. She started as, with a sudden flapping of wings, a bird took off overhead. A bramble scratched her bare legs badly, another clawed at Dennis's shirt.

'You said all our troubles would be over once we reached the cliff top Dennis.' They had entered a glade backed by another towering cliff. Azette eyed it askance. 'I don't care what you say, nothing will make me climb up there.' She stumbled through a stretch of ground elder and lady fern, and threw herself down on a patch of grass.

'You'll feel better after a rest my love,' observed Dennis sitting down beside her and looking up at the fronds of dead ivy which hung from trees like ropes. 'I'll not be surprised to see Tarzan swing from tree to tree on those fronds,' he chuckled.

'I think you'd still find something to laugh at if you were tied to a stake,' she frowned.

'Why so serious?' he asked lightly.

'I don't exactly know, but I feel we've come to the end of something.'

He moved closer to her, and scanned her face with his strange flecked eyes until she was conscious of the warmth of his body, and the heady perfume of the elder flowers. Her feelings for her cousin had undergone a change. Could this be how her mother had once felt for his father? She said half sadly:

'Can we go on getting into foolish scrapes without having any other outlets for our feelings for each other?'

He smoothed her tangled fair hair back from her forehead. 'How do you want it to be?'

'You must know what I mean.'

'No,' he insisted. 'It can't be like that for us.'

'Why not? We are only third cousins.'

'It isn't because of that.'

'Why then?'

He replied evasively, 'I've always had a feeling that we were not meant to be more than friends. We started that way before we could walk, isn't it too late to alter things now?'

She searched his eyes intently for the truth. 'There's another reason isn't there? Tell me?'

He clambered to his feet quickly. 'Let's get moving, the decay and rot of this place is getting me down; besides we're on an ants' nest.'

'I'll not move from here until you tell me everything,' she persisted as she stood up and faced him.

He hesitated, then stressed fiercely, 'Dad doesn't even know this, and I'd slit your throat if you told him or anybody else. The romance between your mother and Dad went all the way. When she found she was going to have his child, he was in the Navy and Jersey was occupied by the Germans.'

'I didn't know,' Azette gasped. 'I never thought their love affair had gone so far. What happened to the baby? It would have been my sister or brother — yours too.' Her hands were trembling.

'Yes, we could have shared a brother or sister if your mother hadn't had a miscarriage after an accident.'

'How do you know all this?'

'That's something I can never tell you,' he told her emphatically. 'But you know I never lie to you Azette.'

'I am sure of that.'

'It's lurked at the back of my mind since I knew. I was in my early teens then, and I used to brood about it a lot. It seemed to make us closer than cousins; you would seem too close to me in fact. I expect that was why I could never make a pass at you.'

Azette studied him with shocked eyes. How her mother must have suffered. Azette fancied that now something left over from their parents' romance was making itself felt between Dennis and herself.

'The fact that my mother conceived your father's child can't mean that you and I must always remain apart.' She was offering him her lips.

'If you say so.' His mouth met hers

tentatively before he kissed her passionately. Afterwards Azette did not feel as elated as she had expected; but then the transition from friends to lovers might be slow. Dennis handed her a broken branch and found one for himself. 'Come on, we shall have to beat our way.'

She followed him as he pushed past countless bamboos. Their movements were less restricted when they stepped out into the open, but then they had the full force of the sun on their heads.

'Pity these blackberries aren't ripe,' Dennis turned to say.

'A pity we missed our ale in the *Sailors' Inn*. Which way? The Caravan Camp, or Warren Woods?'

'We're about mid way between them. Warren Woods are nearer home.'

Without another word, they set off eastwards; their way was torturous, they were scratched by brambles, bitten by mosquitos and stung by nettles. Whenever they thought they had found a pathway, they were warded off by bamboos or held at bay by spiky gorse. Azette was very thirsty and Dennis was very hungry; Azette's canvas shoes had rubbed painful blisters on her bare feet, Dennis had knocked his watch against a rock, it had stopped. Azette had left hers in the flat. When Dennis scrambled up a steep bank using exposed roots for footholds, he cried:

'Thank God, there's a proper footpath up here.' He stretched out his hand to help her.

They trudged on wearily without talking. They swiped at brambles growing across the path, and looked ahead for signs that the jungle was thinning.

'We're nearly there, I know this place; it's Faraway Lane,' Azette uttered thankfully. 'Oh. There's Andrew.'

Andrew was striding through the bracken from the direction of the old oak which blocked the entrance to Faraway Valley. His hair was wet, so he had been swimming. He looked in horror at Azette's tangled hair, her perspiring face, her dirty white T-shirt and shorts, her badly scratched arms and her cut knees.

'Azette! What has happened to you?' Dennis did the explaining.

'And so you climbed that cliff; you might have been killed.' Andrew regarded the cousins furiously. 'My car is at the end of this lane. I'll drive the two of you home.' As Azette limped by his side he asked. 'What's wrong with your foot?'

'It's only a blister,' she dismissed it, but still made use of her stick.

14

Andrew's mouth was set in an angry line after he had dropped Dennis outside the Tollhouse, and was driving Azette down the hill to the town.

'Will Jane be in?' he asked brusquely.

'Not until late.'

'Then I'll make sure you have a meal, and a soak in disinfectant.'

'Sheep Dip?'

'You look as though you need it.'

'I wish you hadn't been so angry when you met us in the woods.'

'I was shattered when I knew you had climbed that cliff.'

'But I've been cliff climbing with Dennis since we were kids.'

Back at the flat Azette agreed with anything Andrew suggested, her whole body ached. She was longing for a cup of tea, but too exhausted to put the kettle on. Andrew did that, then ran her bath and added Dettol. She was horrified when she caught sight of her face in the sitting-room mirror; leaves clung to her hair, her cheeks were scratched and streaked with dust.

'I didn't know I looked like this.'

'You do, but you're still kissable.' Andrew kissed her lightly.

★ ★ ★

Azette was considerably revived when she sat opposite Andrew at the sitting-room table. He knew his way round Jane's kitchenette, and had heated a can of beef broth.

'I'm handy with a tin opener; and I excel at scrambled eggs, they're in the double pan. Biscuits and cheese to follow, oh but I mustn't forget I've put a strawberry ice in the refrig'.'

'Where did that come from?' Azette asked surprised.

'I went out whilst you were in the bath. That sweet shop round the corner

198

was open, I bought this Burgundy from the pub.'

The Burgundy was smooth and at its best; it helped to make Dennis's astounding revelation concerning their parents more bearable. Azette warmed towards Andrew and expressed her gratitude.

'My pleasure.' He gave a half smile, then added more seriously, 'When I was driving past the farmhouse, I wished I could have asked you and Dennis into my home so that you might lick your wounds. I could have told the builders to go ahead months ago.'

'And now?'

Her question hung between them whilst Andrew weighed the matter up.

'I will tell them to go ahead so that the roof will be on before the winter sets in; I will have burnt clay tiles instead of thatch.'

Whilst Andrew made the coffee, Azette switched on Jane's radio; she knew it would please him to listen to Beethoven. Soon after the programme ended, the telephone rang from the landing. Azette answered it and, when she returned her eyes blazed excitedly.

'It was Dennis,' she told Andrew. 'He wanted to know how I was and — '

'Yes?'

'Andrew, I can trust you to keep a secret, which is more than I can say for Jane, and I must tell somebody.'

'Well?'

Azette went back to her place on the settee, and faced Andrew who was seated on an armchair. 'If Dennis's exhibition is a success, he wants me to marry him and live with him in Jersey.' When Andrew passed no comment, but continued to eye her with ill-concealed disapproval, she asked. 'Isn't it great?'

'That remains to be seen,' he responded grimly.

Her face showed her disappointment at his lack of enthusiasm. 'Can't you realize what this will mean to me? After Dennis and I are married, we need never be parted from each other again; the life which we shared as kids will be carried on into eternity.'

'But you and Dennis aren't children any more. I've heard of some odd reasons for wanting to marry a person, but your remark about wanting to carry the life you shared as children into eternity, is the most stupid of all.'

'Andrew!'

'Now don't ask how I dare say that, otherwise I shall dare to tell you much more as well.'

Andrew rose to his feet, turned to the mantelpiece and wound the clock which had stopped.

'Be happy for me Andrew,' Azette pleaded from behind.

'I always want to be able to be happy for you Azette,' he turned back to her to say. 'I don't believe you have any idea how fond of you I have become. I was — ' He broke off as though he had already said too much, and studied the post cards from Jersey which were propped on the mantelpiece. 'Is Mandy still enjoying herself?' he asked.

'So much that my parents persuaded

her to stay on longer. Mrs Stewart had said that Mandy could have leave of absence for as long as she wished. In her last letter Mandy said she would try to book a seat on a plane next week.'

'Is anybody meeting her?'

'No. Michael will be at Poole most of the time.'

'Then I'll meet Mandy; let me know what day.'

★ ★ ★

A constant stream of visitors passed through the double doors of the exhibition hall to view Dennis's works; one by one his paintings bore red tags to indicate they had been sold. Azette was elated; there was no doubt now that she and Dennis would be able to marry. She looked forward to the time when they could set up a home together in Jersey, they would have to make do with some rented property at first. Sometimes she visualized them as living in a small bungalow in Rozel

Bay, other times she could picture them living in a flat in the shadow of Mont Orgueil Castle; but when she was more realistic she realized that they might have to make do with a caravan on the dunes to start off with. No matter, they would be together, and their life would be a continuation of their childhood.

One afternoon she sought out Andrew who had been working since early morning in the cornfield. The sun beat down on the combine harvester, and Azette watched interestedly as it cut the corn, threshed it, laid aside the straw and put the grain into bags.

'I heard from Mandy this morning,' she told Andrew when he crossed the stubble to have a word with her. 'She will fly back next Friday afternoon.'

'I'll be there to meet the plane.'

'Thank you Andrew, it'll be nicer for Mandy to be met by somebody she knows; Jane and I will expect you to have tea with us.' Azette frowned at the straw which appeared to have been cast aside as though useless. 'What about that straw?'

'I shall have it worked back into the soil by a rotator. Don't worry, I'm as practical as you when it comes to farming,' Andrew said teasingly. 'On my father's farm, his poultry are turned into a field like this to eat the fallen grain. We Scottish waste nothing. Have you time to see my dryer at work in the long barn?'

'Just time,' she replied glancing at her watch.

She chatted animatedly as they left the field together. In the barn a dryer was blowing hot air through sacks of grain. Azette was full of praise for its speed, and listened with interest as Andrew spoke of his intention of buying more machinery as time went on. When they had left the barn he asked:

'How is Dennis's exhibition progressing?'

'Marvellously thanks. The press came yesterday, and he is to have a good write-up; Lady Monica has been good at urging all her wealthy friends to attend. Oh, he has sold so many paintings already.'

'Which means he will be able to marry you?'

'Yes. I do wish you could look more pleased for us Andrew.'

He looked startled. 'Sorry, I'm not the sort who goes overboard at the mention of a wedding.'

'I think you are a cynic,' she guessed.

'But I assure you I'm not,' he insisted before they parted.

She thought about him all the way back to Warren House. She could not decide what that undefinable expression in his eyes had meant when they had spoken of Dennis; surely when he said he had become fond of her, he had not meant he was falling in love with her.

★   ★   ★

When Azette opened the door of the flat to Mandy on Friday, she was delighted to see how well and relaxed she looked. Azette longed to hear intimate details about her family, but Andrew was coming up the stairs with Mandy's suitcase and, almost immediately, Jane was calling from behind him:

'Hi, everybody.'

'I've left my heart in Jersey,' Mandy smiled as Andrew set down her case. 'But it's great to be home.' She took a cake box from a plastic carrier. 'Your mother said you liked Jersey Wonders, Azette.'

Before Azette and Jane had left the flat that morning, they had laid the table ready for a salad meal. Now the four of them gathered round, and the girls laughed at Andrew's expression when he tried a Jersey Wonder. Mandy's dark eyes no longer looked out sadly from a pinched pale face, but were peaceful and her once hollow cheeks had filled out. Hitherto she had been inclined to leave talking to others, now she took command of the conversation.

'Your family were so kind Azette. I went to your mother's farm at Portelet, to the Le Bruns' farm at St Brelades' and to tea with Dennis's family in St Helier. Both your brothers drove me round the island, and your parents took me to see the castles when they were floodlit.' Mandy chatted on until they had finished their meal. 'And now,' she proclaimed with an enigmatic smile, 'I will tell you what Azette's mother has persuaded me to do. She said I should tell the baby's father the truth.'

Azette could well imagine her mother giving Mandy that good advice; now that Dennis had told her that her mother once carried a child before marriage, she found it even easier to understand her mother's concern for Mandy.

'Azette's mother is right,' agreed Andrew at once.

'I'm glad you've come to your senses at last, Mandy,' Jane put in.

'It's a pity you waited so long,' Azette declared. 'Never mind, there's still time to marry before the baby is born.'

'Yes,' agreed Mandy. 'I was so silly not to have told the father before. The whole thing was as much my fault as his. We had never met until the night of that party; at first there was drinking, then couples paired off and went to bedrooms. The living-room had a horrid smoky smell, we hadn't thought at first that nearly everyone was smoking Cannabis. It was because we didn't agree with drugs, and because we were immediately attracted to each other, that we paired off. I've always needed some sort of comfort since my mother died, but that sounds a foolish excuse for going to bed with a stranger.'

'No, it doesn't sound foolish,' stated Andrew. 'Things like that happen all the time don't they? The foolish thing about it was that you took no precautions,' he finished bluntly.

Mandy fluttered her slim hands distressfully. 'But I didn't know much about sex.' Mandy explored the past months. 'When I was sure I was to have a baby, I hadn't a clue what to do. The father had gone to London; any way I thought I couldn't expect a comparative stranger to marry me. So I hoped that one day I'd wake up and find it was all a dream, and that I wasn't pregnant.'

'You must write to this chap if he is in London,' Jane insisted.

'He's back in Tollbury now,' explained Mandy quietly. 'I've seen him once and he seemed to like me quite a lot, but I hadn't the right sort of courage to tell him how things were, I didn't want him to feel trapped.'

'That's typically you, Mandy, always thinking of others before yourself,' Jane smiled at her fondly. 'But now you will tell him as soon as possible?'

Whilst Mandy and Jane were debating this point, Andrew was watching Azette in concern; he noted how the blood slowly drained from her face.

Jane was saying, 'I can't say how he will feel, not knowing him, Mandy.'

'But you *do* know him Jane. He is Dennis. It's because Azette's mother knows him so well that she said he would want to marry me, she thought we were made for each other.'

Andrew regarded Azette in alarm now; her face appeared to be graven from stone. He had to think of an excuse to get her out of the room, he said:

'I forgot to tell Curtis I would not be back for dinner; Azette you can pacify him better than I can. Come to the 'phone with me.'

Whilst Mandy was intent on asking Jane if she thought Dennis would be difficult to approach, Andrew had contrived to pull Azette's chair back from the table. She moved as though in a trance, but he caught hold of her arm; they were soon crossing the sands together. When they halted behind a breakwater, she gave a sad sigh which went right to his heart.

'I think my mother has betrayed me.'

'Surely not. Did you write to tell her you were going to marry Dennis?'

'No. We were to wait until his

exhibition closed. I told nobody but you Andrew.' Her lips trembled. 'How could Mum say that Mandy and Dennis were meant for each other? He was meant for *me*.'

'Mothers have a way of knowing what is best for their children,' Andrew observed gently. 'You may not want to believe this has happened to you, Azette, but it has, and you must face up to it.'

'I shall never let Dennis go,' she vowed obstinately.

'I believe you have felt like that since the time when you first walked into some childish trouble with him, and found it was fun.'

'Perhaps. But *I* have known Dennis all my life.'

'You have made your point. You saw Dennis first, therefore you think you have first claim on him.'

'Yes.'

'Even though Mandy expects his child?'

'Yes.'

'Be reasonable Azette. Either you or Mandy must be hurt over this.'

'And who do you think it will be?' asked Azette icily.

'That rests with Dennis doesn't it?'

'Is every man who puts a girl in the family way expected to marry her?'

'Not if he can't love her. But at least play fair, and stand back to give Dennis a chance to decide what he wants to do.'

'But Dennis is mine.'

'Don't be absurd. You can't own a man.'

15

The next morning Azette awoke to the realization that life went on whatever her personal sufferings might be. Jane was looking out of the window at the ropes of gay flags looped between the lamp-posts on the promenade. It was Regatta Saturday and she was caught up by its carefree mood. She switched on her record player, and was disinclined to talk about anything but the prospects of *The Swift* winning the race for which Michael had entered. Jane was to crew for him. Azette tried to show interest, but all she could think of was Mandy's surprising disclosure of yesterday. She went about her usual Saturday morning chores mechanically whilst wondering what Dennis's attitude to Mandy was going to be.

In the afternoon Azette and Mandy joined the crowds lined up on the harbour. The wind was southerly which was ideal for fast sailing; when Michael's race commenced at the crack of the starting gun, Azette's eyes never left *The Swift*. It was streaking ahead of the other entries. Michael was an expert helmsman, and Jane was sitting out in the way only one experienced in crewing can do. They formed an ideal team; they led all the way and won the cup.

'Jane and Michael make a great couple,' Mandy enthused. 'Their 'off, on' relationship seems to be 'on' now.'

'I wonder how long for,' Azette mused.

Earlier that week there had been trouble between the couple when Jane had made disparaging remarks about her uncle; then Michael had been quick to stress how very courageous he was when they had been lost in the thick mist whilst fishing. Michael had told Jane it was time she rid herself of the idea that anybody over forty was too square, and useless to deserve a place on earth. Jane flounced off after saying Michael could find someone else to crew for him. However, soon she had sought Michael out to apologize.

'When Jane is ready to settle down, perhaps she will marry Michael,' thought Mandy.

'Perhaps,' agreed Azette tersely. Her nerves were edgy. 'But a girl can't count on marrying until a man puts a wedding ring on her finger. Are you counting on Dennis asking you to marry him?'

'We must do what is best for the baby,' Mandy answered softly. 'But we must find out if we can love each other first.'

Azette found it impossible to say anything to hurt such a sweet natured girl as Mandy. But last evening when she had told Andrew she would never give Dennis up, she had meant it. Mandy slid her slim hand through Azette's arm as they walked back down the crowded harbour. A child was racing towards them, his mother pulled him away from Mandy's path respecting her condition; Mandy smiled her thanks at the mother, and their eyes met as though sharing the joy of her condition. Azette bit her lip, she could not help being envious of the girl who was carrying Dennis's child. Mandy unconsciously added to her misery by saying:

'I feel so peaceful today, Azette; when the baby moves I think of Dennis. I'm sure everything will turn out all right.'

★   ★   ★

In the evening a circle of stalls was erected on the sands where a ram was being roasted; a crowd of local residents, and dozens of holiday makers, quickly gathered. When darkness fell the first fireworks were released from the harbour; rockets shot upwards then green, pink, red and gold stars fell into the dark water. Further out Azette saw the even flicker of a lightship. There came a dramatic moment when the fishing boats sailed out of the harbour; each was brightly illuminated. They sailed slowly round the dark bay as gracefully as swans keeping an equal distance from each other, and expressing a leisured air. Afterwards Azette looked around the crowded beach for Dennis, he was nowhere to be seen, but then his exhibition kept open later on Saturday evenings. Mandy had not had a chance to speak to him yet; until she did Dennis would still be thinking of her as being his future wife. Azette clung to that thought.

People jostled each other for a turn at the hoop-la stall, they ate winkles, hot dogs, toffee apples and candy floss. Azette and Mandy crossed to a huge bonfire which had been lit by youths from drift-wood. A cream slit appeared in the black sky, it widened quickly as the moon came up; but the area surrounding the bonfire was in shadow. Laughter and merry voices were louder than the splash of the waves; on the far side of the fire faces would suddenly stand out boldly when caught in the movement of a flame.

Then through the flames Azette saw Dennis, and she longed to go to him, but Mandy had already left her side; a flame, larger than the rest, united Dennis's cheerful face and Mandy's soulful one; the flame flickered and died down and they were lost in the shadows. A youth threw more wood on the fire and the flames rose high again, but Mandy and Dennis had gone. Azette was alone.

She mingled aimlessly with the crowd unconsciously seeking a friendly face, but they were all strangers to her, and Michael and Jane had gone to celebrate at the Yacht Club. Soon she saw Andrew standing on the steps of the *Sailors' Inn*; he was talking to members of the Speed Boat Club and did not notice her. A girl stood either side of him, one of them rested her hand on his broad shoulder; Azette hastily dodged behind a deck chair hut and made her way to the promenade. She pulled up sharply when she saw Mandy and Dennis passing under an archway of coloured lights; they walked slowly hand-in-hand and she could guess what they spoke of.

She turned back and walked straight into a crowd of Jane's unpleasant looking friends who slept rough in the shelters; Michael had repeatedly warned Jane against them, besides being heavy drinkers he suspected they took drugs. Now they called to Azette to join them, they waved bottles and cracked lewd jokes. Azette squeezed past them, but one youth (known as 'The Lion' because of his mane of yellow hair) followed her; his clothing smelt of stale sweat. She shot up a steep lane and hid in a doorway until satisfied he had given up the chase.

She walked on up the hill where the chirrups of the bush crickets reminded her of her home in Jersey. She longed to be with her parents and her brothers again; she was lonely here on this quiet hillside, but if she re-joined the crowd milling round the harbour, she might walk straight into Dennis and Mandy, or she might be accosted again by The Lion. And so she walked on slowly and passed waste ground where the night whispered through bracken like the voice of a woman. It reminded Azette of the times when her mother had shared whispered confidences with her. What would her mother have said had she known that Dennis had promised to marry her? Would she still have advised Mandy to tell him her secret? The wind blew with renewed force, and sighed through heather like a woman in sorrow.

★ ★ ★

Dennis telephoned Azette early the following day. His exhibition was closed on Sunday mornings; she must meet him on an isolated beach so they might have a private talk. She had no need to ask what he wished to talk about.

Dennis appeared to be stricken with

remorse when he crossed the sands to her. By mutual consent, they headed eastwards; they splashed through rock-pools, and passed exposed rocks where the mottled brown plumage of young gulls mingled with the white and pale grey of the parent birds.

Suddenly Dennis eased his pace and said, 'I must say I was shaken last evening when Mandy told me she was expecting my child. We should have kept away from that party, it wasn't our scene, but we didn't know that at first. The drinks were strong, and we'd taken too much before we realized it. There was a cannabis get-together, we'd no intention of being involved in that — then we found ourselves in an empty bedroom.' With an unexpected move-ment Dennis sprang over a rock, he landed in a shallow pool but carried on walking beside Azette as though noth-ing had happened. 'I'm not trying to excuse myself for what took place, Azette. Soon I'll have a kid to support.'

'Yes, you will have to give Mandy a

proper allowance.' (Dennis had not mentioned marrying Mandy, Azette hoped they had come to some other arrangement.)

'Do you think that is enough?' Dennis asked fiercely. 'If I gave the baby all I possessed, it could not make up to it for being illegitimate.'

'Then what do you propose to do about it?' Azette's voice was cold.

'Don't you think I ought to put the baby first and offer to marry Mandy?' Dennis eyed Azette contritely. 'I feel an awful heel suggesting this after I'd promised to marry you.'

Azette stopped by a comfortable looking rock. 'Let's sit down for a while,' she suggested tiredly.

'It's early in the day for you to feel tired,' he mentioned.

'I'm mentally tired,' she told him. 'We're in a spot Dennis. A far worse spot than we've been in before,' she sighed. 'Well now, we must think what can be done for the best. This awful thing must have been brewing up for us since my first day in Tollbury; I was dreaming that I was on a Jersey beach with you, then waves engulfed you, and I lost you. A warning rocket woke me, and Jane ran to the harbour to find out what had happened. Meanwhile Mandy came in to share my early tea; she told me about the baby, and I told her I had come to find you, Dennis. How ironical it is that you should be its father.' Azette's hazel eyes had a haunted look as she re-lived that morning. 'When Jane came back she said Terry Guard had fallen out of the pebble pickers' boat, neither Jane nor I had a clue that Terry was really you.'

Dennis had listened to his cousin with a strained expression whilst his fingers were moving impatiently, and his feet tapping the sands restlessly. 'You're too fanciful for such a practical person Azette. Now to get down to brass tacks — what are we going to do?'

'What do you *want* to do?'

'I don't have to tell you that I love you, you must know that, but I suppose

I could fall in love with Mandy too if it came to the pinch.'

'Came to the pinch!' Azette echoed sharply.

Dennis ran his fingers worriedly through his hair. 'Given time to get to know each other, Mandy and I might fall in love; of course it wouldn't be the same sort of love as ours, Azette, that was something rather special wasn't it?'

'Do you mean *wasn't* it or *isn't* it?'

'Don't confuse me for God's sake. What I really want to say is that I could only marry Mandy if you released me from my promise to marry you.'

'And if I refused to release you?'

'Then I'd have to think again wouldn't I? I've never broken a promise to you yet.'

'That's so.' Azette tilted her chin determinedly. '*I* can give you children Dennis.'

'Ah God, I don't want to father any more at present. But even if I didn't marry Mandy I would want to see the kid; it has my blood in its veins — come to that it has some of your blood too. If I could learn to love Mandy in time, I could marry her before the baby was born, and take them back to Jersey with me.'

Azette slid off the rock and faced her cousin with angry eyes. 'I was the one who was going back to Jersey with you — remember?'

'I can hardly forget that can I?' Dennis reached out for Azette's hands. 'You don't seem to realize what a devil of a position I'm in; I must think of that baby.'

'There is a chance that Mandy will marry somebody else,' Azette hedged. 'She's a very sweet girl.'

'But I'd not want another man to father my child.' Dennis left the rock and ran his hands up Azette's arms to her shoulders. 'I'd have given anything to have spared you this. I hate hurting you my love.'

'And I hate hurting Mandy,' Azette said wretchedly. 'But I don't feel able

225

to release you from your promise to marry me, Dennis. Can't you see that our future happiness is at stake? What about our plans to make a home in Jersey together? Remember how it used to be with us when we were kids? The good times we had in the summer on the beaches, our walks over the heath, our Christmas parties and the fun we had at family gatherings simply because we were together?'

'Of course I remember everything,' Dennis agreed nostalgically. 'The good times we had together would fill a book.'

'Yes. Surely we can't be expected to close that book and put it away forgotten?'

'Oh God, I don't know,' Dennis frowned. 'I've often thought you could dominate me, Azette, on a major issue; please don't try to do that now. And please don't rush me. I've not had time to think rationally. That's what I need — more time.'

'More time to see Mandy I suppose,' Azette uttered curtly.

She turned away, and he regarded the footprints she had left in the sand helplessly.

16

During the following weeks Dennis devoted his spare time to getting to know Mandy. Azette saw nothing of him, she kept her feelings under control, and succeeded in carrying on with her work at Warren House in her usual calm manner. Only Andrew was aware of her intense misery. She tried not to bother him with her troubles whilst his thoughts were on ensilage, the problems of installing new electric wiring and the late ripening of the oats. There was also the task of moving the sheep down from the hills to clear a pasture.

Early one afternoon Azette was walking down a lane, where musk thistle brightened the grassy banks with its crimson flower-heads, and nuts were ripening in the hedges, when she heard the sound of a concrete mixer. The rebuilding of Warren Farmhouse was underway. She watched men unload bricks from a lorry whilst others worked on the original foundations of the old house.

'I shall have to charge you entertainment tax, Azette.' Andrew had stepped from behind the lorry to discuss his plans for the new farmhouse with Azette. All the while he studied her face worriedly. 'How are things going between you and Dennis?'

'They are not 'going' at all; I have only seen him once since Mandy came home. His exhibition is to stay open for an extra two weeks, and his evenings are taken up with Mandy. He — he wants to find out if they can fall in love.'

'And then?'

'If they can, I shall be expected to free Dennis from his promise to marry me.'

'Is it going to be very difficult for you to do that?' Andrew asked gently.

'Almost impossible.'

'Even when there is the baby to consider?'

'Even then.'

Andrew cupped his hand round her elbow, and led her back to the lane where the nuts grew.

'It's up to you to release Dennis if he asks you, but, of course, it may not come to that. Are you sure you're not hanging on to him purely because you associate him with your past happiness; I realize he represents all the fun and excitement you had when you were kids, but for heaven's sake snap out of it, and look to your future instead Azette.'

'I can have no future without Dennis.'

'Now you are being dramatic. You are young and lovely, there will be dozens of other men.'

'I don't want dozens of them,' she protested pettishly.

'Well then — there could be one other man.'

'How can you tell that?'

'It's not very difficult, you're so attractive and sweet. But do be reasonable.'

'Dennis and I so often had mishaps when we were out together, but we always recovered from them. But, after he had pulled me out of some quicksands, I was afraid that one day something terrible might happen from which we could not free ourselves. It *has* happened, but not in the way I expected at all.'

'It is the unexpected troubles that hit us, not those over which we've worried.' Andrew paused by a gate leading into a pasture. 'I'll walk back this way with you, then we can see how the sheep like the new grazing.'

The flock's fleece had commenced to grow again, they presented a fine sight with their proudly curving horns and dark ringed eyes. The black and white Welsh sheepdog growled and bared his teeth at Andrew and Azette.

'He's not exactly friendly is he?' Andrew remarked. 'Still he knows his job,' he added as the dog raced backwards and forwards, and barked warningly to keep the sheep from moving across to the gate which Andrew was having difficulty in closing.

Azette was thinking of the evening when Andrew had driven her up to the hills to see the flock before the shearing. It had been a lovely evening, and how light-hearted she had felt then compared with now.

'Where is Mr Yaffle?' she asked.

'Away on holiday. This is a good time for him to go. It is easy for me to keep an eye on the sheep down here, and Green feeds the sheepdog.'

'The oats are still not ripe,' Azette observed as they passed through a second gateway, and took a narrow path between the oats and a small wood.

'No, it's disappointing, but then a certain amount of sun is cut off by that wooded area, also the sowing was late due to that rainy spell.' Andrew gave an angry exclamation. 'What on the hell are those louts doing in the wood?'

Andrew pushed his way through scrub to where two young men were erecting a rough tent. Azette frowned on recognizing the yellow haired youth, he was 'The Lion', and his brown haired companion was another member of his gang. They protested loudly when Andrew gave them their marching orders.

'We weren't doing any harm,' grumbled The Lion. 'We needed a change of air.'

'Don't hope to find that on my land,' Andrew thundered.

'Oh come off it,' cried the brown haired youth. He glanced up at the spreading branches of an oak appreciatively. 'I bet you don't know what it is like to be without a roof over your head.'

This was an unfortunate remark, it unintentionally stabbed at Andrew like a knife. He advanced and grabbed the youths by their collars.

'If you don't dismantle that apology for a tent immediately, I'll knock your heads together.' It was clear that

Andrew meant it.

'All right, all right,' quavered The Lion who appeared to have shrunk considerably since he had pestered Azette on Regatta night. 'We're going.'

Andrew spread out his strong arms, and cast the youths aside as though they were empty sacks.

★ ★ ★

Jane was eager to talk about Mandy and Dennis whilst sharing her evening meal with Azette that night.

'Did you hear what happened to Mandy late last evening, Azette?'

'No?'

'Dennis took her to the cinema and, when they were leaving, she slipped down some stairs.'

'Oh. Was she hurt?' Azette asked in alarm.

'No, but Dennis insisted on taking her to the doctor's round the corner. He gave Mandy a thorough examination then assured her the baby could not have come to any harm.' Jane giggled. 'Mandy said Dennis was the one who needed a doctor, he was frantic with worry over Mandy and the baby. I believe he has fallen for Mandy. Let's hope he marries her.'

Azette made some suitable reply, and wondered how much longer it would be before Dennis was in touch with her again. Mandy tapped at the door and entered then. She carried a skirt of Azette's and told her with a triumphant smile, 'Didn't I promise you I could invisibly mend that tear?' She crossed to the window to hold the tweed skirt up to the light. 'I removed threads from the seam, and used them for darning.'

Whilst Mandy and Azette were studying the skirt, they were unaware that a smartly dressed woman in her late forties stood in the doorway talking to Jane. She was saying, 'Oh there you are Jane. I had no reply when I rang Mandy's bell although her door was open; when I heard voices, I thought she must be with you.'

Jane hesitated uncomfortably, it was too late to pretend that Mandy was out when she clearly visible. She announced quite needlessly:

'Here's your step-mother, Mandy.'

'Hullo Cara,' Mandy smiled wanly. If Azette had not been holding the skirt she could have made use of it to camouflage her swollen stomach. Her slim fingers moved helplessly, then finally came to rest on Azette's arm. 'This is Azette,' she said lamely.

'I am pleased to meet you Azette.' The three girls waited unhappily for what was to come next; Cara could not have failed to be unaware of her step-daughter's condition, but she had not battered an eyelid. 'I called on chance to see you Mandy; your father and I have been very worried about you recently, it did seem you were avoiding us when we 'phoned to ask you out.' Her sharp eyes travelled downwards from Mandy's startled face to her pink smock.

Mandy licked her lips, then said

softly, 'Now you can see why I have avoided you Cara.'

'Yes, Mandy; I can see, too, why on the last two occasions that we called on you, you were supposedly ill, and received us in bed under a voluminous eiderdown.'

Jane broke the ensuing silence by saying, 'Let's all sit down, and have a cup of tea. I was going to make another pot,' she finished with forced brightness.

Cara chose one of the armchairs, and Mandy sat opposite to her; Azette placed the small table ready to receive the tea tray, then she sat down on the settee. When Jane had handed round the tea, Cara questioned in an unruffled tone:

'Are you going to marry the baby's father Mandy?'

'I'm not sure yet. I — you see we wanted time to find out if we loved each other first.'

'An excellent idea.' Cara was peeling off her white gloves methodically, the girls watched as one after the other her fingers were freed. 'And *do* you love each other?' The gloves were laid side by side on an expensive skin handbag.

'I'm quite certain that I love him, but he hasn't said if he loves me yet.'

Azette struggled to remain calm at this enlightening news; she took a sip of tea whilst waiting for Cara to speak again.

'And if he can't love you Mandy, what will you do then?' Cara asked.

'I shall keep the baby whatever happens. I have the money that Mum left me, and Mrs Stewart will give me sewing to do in my flat; she pays me very well, especially for smocking.' Mandy shot a defiant look at Cara. 'Nobody can take my baby from me.'

'My dear girl, why should anybody try to do that?'

'I thought you and Dad might — '

Cara set down her tea cup. 'I am the last person to want to take a baby from its mother, I know just what it could mean. May I smoke Jane?' She lit a cigarette and puffed a delicate cloud of smoke up to the ceiling. 'I was expecting a child once by my first husband, we were elated but it was still born. They said I could never have another child; soon after that my husband died, and so I took on a job to try to forget. Those years were very lonely for me Mandy until I met your father. When he asked me to marry him, I looked forward to taking care of you both. I think I have made life easier for your father, but you have always kept me at a distance Mandy. Perhaps you thought I was trying to take your mother's place, but I would never have presumed to do that.'

'I'm sorry Cara. I did not know — I was afraid.'

'I can understand that. I know you young people have this thing about the generation gap, but surely we could be friends Mandy?' Cara stubbed her cigarette out. 'Whether you decide to marry or not, I will always be ready to help you and the baby. Your bedroom is waiting for you, there is plenty of room for your baby too.'

Mandy visibly brightened, and thanked Cara gratefully. Jane was smiling in relief, and Azette's heart was beating faster. Here was a wonderful solution to Mandy's problem. When Dennis knew that she would not have to face the future alone, he would surely realize there was now no need for him to marry Mandy.

★　★　★

'Have you taken root?'

Azette started up from the carpet of wild thyme which grew on the slopes of Faraway Cove. Andrew was standing above her, his arms akimbo and his mouth unsmiling. She sat up and curled her knees under her.

'Andrew I hope you are not angry because I came here, but it's so peaceful.' Azette added desperately. 'I just had to find a place where I could think.'

'Are things as bad as that?' His

annoyance had given way to concern.

'They have been, but they may become better. Last evening Mandy's step-mother called unexpectedly; we thought she was going to be very angry when she discovered Mandy was pregnant, but she took it wonderfully well. She ended up by assuring Mandy that, if she didn't marry, both she and the baby would be welcome to live at home with her and Mandy's father. That would be a wonderful solution wouldn't it?'

'If you think so.'

'Can't you see what it would mean to Dennis and me? If we could always be together, I would be willing to go out to work to help send Mandy an allowance for the baby.'

'And what does Dennis think about all that?'

'I don't know. I haven't seen him yet.'

'Then the most sensible thing is for you to get together to review the whole situation isn't it?'

'I guess you are right.' Azette

scrambled to her feet and faced Andrew. 'What do you think we ought to do?'

'I'm afraid I can't advise you any more about that matter.'

'Oh. Why?'

'If I urged you to release Dennis, one day you might say I had done that because I wanted you for myself.'

His explanation was too brief for her to understand him fully. She studied his face in growing concern; he had not been at the luncheon table, and now she wondered if there was trouble on his farm; he looked tired and worried.

'I've been talking too much about myself, Andrew; something has gone wrong on the farm hasn't it?'

'Yes, very wrong. Last night the sheep got out of that pasture, and invaded the oat field.'

'You mean somebody accidentally left the gate open?' cried Azette in horror.

'It was not an accident. The gate was propped wide open with a piece of rock. When I passed that way this morning, the flock were still tramping over the oats; it was a terrible sight. I suspected those boys were responsible so I 'phoned the police. When I told them how vicious that sheepdog is, they asked the hospital if anybody had been in to have a dog bite treated.'

'And had they?'

'Those two hobos had been bitten badly, and had been given anti-tetanus jabs. It's easy to visualize what happened. Those drop-outs saw a chance to get their own back because I wouldn't let them camp on my land; they propped the gate open and drove the sheep through. The dog must have attacked them. Those sheep were in my care whilst Yaffle was on holiday, I blame myself for not being more alert — first the farmhouse, now this.'

'Don't blame yourself, Andrew, please. You can't be everywhere at once. The police will soon catch up with The Lion.'

'What good will that do?'

She could not answer, but, now

forgetting her own problems, attempted to console Andrew. She reminded him of the ups and downs of a farmer's life, and she spoke of the satisfaction there was when he overcame obstacles. When she noticed him looking broodingly towards the sea, she asked:

'Aren't you going swimming? I have to go back to work now.'

He turned and gave her a rueful smile. 'I'd rather walk back with you than swim alone today. You talk sense Azette, and you have a calming effect on me.'

17

That evening when Azette left Warren House her heart leapt on seeing Dennis's car standing outside the gate. He was pacing restlessly up and down, but halted directly she called his name. Even the shadows cast by the trees could not conceal his pinched look, and the dark shades under his eyes.

'You have been ill,' she cried in concern.

'Not ill, I've not been sleeping well, that's all. Come and have a drink, then we can talk. I've remembered to ring Jane, by the way, to tell her you wouldn't be back.'

Azette did not notice what roads Dennis took, she only noticed there was no sun, and the sky had a dull, grey look; a large cloud, resembling a hawk, seemed to be following them. She did not take in the name of the Inn where they stopped, she was vaguely aware that geese (or ducks?) were painted on the inn sign. The barmaid had a large mouth and smiled often, the table where they sat was glass topped, they drank ale and ate Cornish Pasties and crisps. Then they were back in the sports car and bowling down a lane lined with conifers, they crossed a bridge which spanned a lively river; it carried broken branches as it raced to its destination. Dennis drove over a cattle grid, and soon they were standing on a vast expanse of moorland. It was their kind of country, and they took a track leading past furze and blackberry bushes.

'The berries are ripening,' observed Azette.

'So you'd say every August in Jersey.'

They walked through heather until Azette rested her hand on a slab of rock shaped like an ice-berg. It felt cold and offered no welcome, but they could not walk on indefinitely.

'What is that weird cry?' asked Dennis.

246

'A curlew. Miss Marley has taught me to recognize bird calls.' Azette clasped her hands together agitatedly. 'Well Dennis, what are you going to do?'

He hesitated before saying, 'I want to do my best for everybody, but whatever I do means somebody will be hurt.'

'There is a solution — '

'What?'

'Yesterday Mandy's step-mother called. She was very nice and told Mandy that she, and the baby, could make their home with her and Mandy's father if she did not marry.'

'That's decent of her, but you know as well as I do it could only be second best as far as the baby is concerned. I want the very best for my child.'

Azette moved away from Dennis and stood looking unhappily at the distant horizon above which storm clouds had gathered. There was a conifer forest, whilst, in the middle distance, a farm was built in a sheltered position; the trees growing at its gates could be larch.

Azette was sure the farmer and his wife must be very cosy, perhaps they sat by a kitchen range. She shivered, a keen wind was blowing across the moor where there were no trees, or hedges, to modify its violence. Rabbits ran out from the shelter of bracken, they paused and listened, then raced past some hummocks, but the smallest one was left behind. If sniffed the air uncertainly unable to summon courage to follow its mother. Azette clapped her hands softly to startle it sufficiently to catch up with its family. She thought of young animals, of the tender bleating of a lamb, the appealing ways of a kitten, the helplessness of a newly born puppy, the high pitched cry of a baby hedgehog and the antics of the white kids on her father's farm. Mandy's unborn child was as defenceless as they were. Azette knew what she had to do then, perhaps she had known all along, but had not wanted to admit it. She crossed the heather to Dennis, her head erect, her movements certain.

'Dennis, I am going to release you from your promise to marry me because I know, deep in my heart, it is the right thing to do. I guess nobody gets by if they go against their conscience.'

'I shall find it almost impossible to let you go Azette, you've always been a part of my life.'

'And you have always been a part of mine, Dennis, but that is all in the past now.'

'All right, all right, don't start telling me that life must go on will you.'

'Very well, I won't. You will not find it hard to love Mandy I'm sure; but you must have found that out by now.'

'Yes, I could love Mandy, and will do my best to make a go of it. But you — ' He held out his arms to her and she went into them with a sad little sigh.

'I will keep right out of your way Dennis to make it easier for you, for us both. Mandy must never know about us.'

'I shall never tell her or anybody else.'

He smoothed back her hair and kissed her brow. 'I always knew you and I weren't meant to love each other. We were too close.'

'Can lovers be too close?'

He made no reply. The wind tore up to them and blew Azette's hair forward so that it framed Dennis's face. She wound her arms round his neck when he kissed her with increasing desperation. Suddenly she freed herself from his arms, and forced herself to cry lightly:

'I'll race you back to the car Dennis.'

Thinking to please her, and knowing it could be the last of the many races they had run together, he slowed his steps to allow her to win.

★ ★ ★

'Good grief!' protested Michael. 'You're not going to wear that at Mandy's wedding.'

Jane flashed him an impish smile, and paraded round her sitting-room.

250

'But that's one of Mandy's new smocks,' cried Azette. 'You must be joking.'

The yellow smock had not been washed, and the dressing caused it to stand out stiffly.

'You look twelve months pregnant,' protested Michael in horror.

'Good. That's how I want to look Michael. I know Mandy feels wretched at having to appear before the Registrar so obviously preggy. If her bridesmaid looks preggy too, she isn't going to feel so sensitive is she?'

'You can carry loyalty too far,' Michael gasped. 'I don't know — ' He was considering Jane's odd behaviour, suddenly he laughed and caught hold of her before she could return to her bedroom. 'At times like this, Jane, I can only love you.' He kissed her fondly.

Azette did not know whether she wanted to laugh or to cry. In a few days now Dennis and Mandy would be married; she must remain outwardly cheerful until then.

'A lucky thing that Dennis's exhibition was such a howling success,' remarked Michael returning to his armchair and accepting a cup of coffee from Azette. 'I expect his folks will give him a great reception when he goes back to Jersey. Will Mandy go with him?'

'No, the doctor has advised her to stay on the mainland until the baby is born — it won't be long now. Her step-mother wants her to go back to her home until then so that she can keep an eye on her.'

'Best idea,' agreed Michael. 'Does Dennis want to settle in Jersey for good?'

'I think so, if he can find himself somewhere to live; that won't be easy, but the family have lots of contacts out there.'

Azette hoped she would not feel so bad once Dennis and Mandy were married; there would be a finality about everything, and there would be no more living on false hopes. The wedding would be a frightful ordeal of course but afterwards she could go away by herself and have a good cry, or she could blow her week's wages on some extravagant thing, or she could go for a hike and walk until she dropped.

⋆ ⋆ ⋆

The weather turned very warm and the temperature rose steadily.

'I wish I could spend all day in the sea,' Azette observed whilst she ate a hurried breakfast with Jane the day before Mandy's wedding.

Jane was reading a letter from her father, and was looking unusually concerned. 'Dad says Mum hasn't been well. They are due to return to England for good the autumn after next; now Dad wants Mum to come back ahead of him, but she insists on sticking it out. Their nearest neighbours have left, they must be very lonely.' Jane pushed the remains of her breakfast aside. 'Parents seem more human when they are in trouble.' She glanced at the clock. 'Don't miss your 'bus Azette.'

At Warren House the Professor had thrown his study window wide open.

'What an airless day; however it will be cool in the church. I have to escort my sisters to that blasted wedding this afternoon Azette.' He looked over his glasses at her. 'You seem under the weather. You can push off after luncheon.'

Luncheon was served early so that the Marleys could arrive at the church on time. As Andrew had driven to Dorchester on business, Lady Monica and her sister monopolized the conversation during the meal. What would the bride wear? Would the groom have had his hair cut? Azette listened unhappily, tomorrow she would have to watch Dennis marrying Mandy. She wondered how she could face up to the ceremony. She closed the study windows after the Marleys had driven off to the church, then covered her typewriter and tidied her desk. She had already missed a 'bus into Tollbury, now it would be more than two hours before she could have her swim — unless she swam in Faraway Cove.

Bees were hovering over the wild thyme in the little valley, and a soft wind was moving the leaves of the palm. This was the place where the rare orchid grew, where the brook sang as it babbled past banks of rich grasses and where the air seemed to have a healing quality.

The tide was high, Azette crossed a fringe of white sand, left her clothes on a rock and plunged naked into the sea. Gentle waves caressed her warm skin, she felt soothed as she twisted and turned in the refreshing salt water. When she became aware that Andrew was swimming into the cove, she was spinning round like a top; she had to do something idiotic if she was not going to break down and cry. Andrew lapsed into a side stroke and circled her without speaking, his eyes were on her critically. She stilled her movements and asked sharply:

'Well aren't you going to say anything Andrew?'

'You are the first girl who has made me speechless.'

'Oh. Why?'

'I warned you not to come here because I like to swim without a costume, but here you are as stark as I am, but twice as beautiful; further more you are behaving like an idiot.'

She sobered down completely. 'I thought you were in Dorchester; the Marleys went to a wedding so the Professor gave me the afternoon off. I missed the Tollbury 'bus so came here for a swim.'

'Why not go down to Warren Beach?'

'I did not have a swim suit.'

He gave a curt laugh. 'What's the matter with you? You look almost wild.'

'I feel wild. I had to do something crazy or I should have cried myself sick. I have to go to a wedding myself tomorrow. Dennis and Mandy are getting married.'

'I didn't know about that.' He had stopped circling her and was treading water.

'I didn't feel up to talking about it any more.'

'So you finally released Dennis from his promise?'

'Yes, but I only did it for the baby's sake.'

'It was the best thing you could do. Surely Dennis doesn't expect you to be at his wedding?'

'No, but as nobody, but you, knows that I was to marry him, I couldn't think of an excuse not to go.' She pushed her wet hair from her face and regarded Andrew with tortured eyes.

'That wedding is definitely out for you Azette. Now what excuse can you give?' Andrew eyed Azette thoughtfully. 'Ah, I know. You are to drive down to Cornwall with me. I asked you weeks ago to meet my parents. Remember?'

'Yes.' She looked at him doubtfully. 'But we can't land on them unexpectedly.'

'I will 'phone them directly we reach the house; my mother has already written to say she looks forward to meeting you.'

'But I must be back at work on Monday morning. How soon can we go?'

'We could leave within the hour.' He thought quickly. 'I'll find Boy, pack, square it with Posser and Green, drive you to Tollbury where you will pack whilst I fill up with petrol. How's that?'

'Quite crazy. My hair is wet and — '

'But you said you wanted to do something crazy.'

★ ★ ★

Mandy had left a basket outside her front door for the baker; Azette was thankful she was out, she would not have to make her apologies. She could write to her later, and now telephone Jane to explain why she would be away for the weekend. Jane had an understanding with Azette that if she was

258

busy at her reception desk, she would cut her short when telephoning. This afternoon she must have had the reception office to herself; she was eager to gossip. She exclaimed when Azette told her she was going to the Gordons' farm.

'You must be mad Azette.'

'Why?' queried Azette. 'Andrew said a long time ago that he wanted me to meet his parents, and see over their farm.'

'Has he told you he's married?'

'Of course not.'

'Then he should have told you.'

'But I thought your Aunt Monica was hoping you would marry him Jane?'

'She was. That's a great laugh really. Those Cornish girls who were passing through Tollbury with Jerry's crowd told me — they were at Andrew's wedding.'

Azette concealed her surprise. 'There's nothing wrong in being married is there?' she asked sharply.

'No, provided you don't fall for Andrew.'

'I won't.' Azette had no intention of risking another unhappy love affair. 'Where is Andrew's wife?'

'Haven't a clue. I bet he wanted to keep it quiet, so I kept my mouth shut.'

'That must have been painful for you.'

Jane pretended not to hear Azette's acid comment, and carried on, 'Perhaps Andrew's bride was like the mad wife in *Jane Eyre*, and was killed when his farmhouse caught fire. I must cut off now Azette. Good-bye.'

Azette had packing to do, she did not have time to think over what Jane had told her until Andrew was driving towards Devon. Jane thought the world of Mandy, it was possible she had said Andrew was married to prevent Azette going to Cornwall and so missing Mandy's wedding. But if Andrew was married it was his own concern; he had obviously not intended her to take the few kisses they had exchanged seriously. After she had told him she was to marry Dennis, he had never made a pass at her; most surely when she met his family she would learn his true state.

'My father's parents lived near Exeter,' she observed as they passed through that town.

'I thought your Jersey farm had been their home.'

'It was until the last war. My grandfather was a soldier at heart, not a farmer; he fought in the first war and trained soldiers near Exeter in the second. He was a humorous old man, great fun; grandmother was sweet and placid; when he died, she lost the will to live.' Andrew listened with interest when Azette told him more about her Renouf grandparents. 'Where are we going now Andrew?' she asked.

'Through Mortonhampstead, then across Dartmoor. That should please you.'

Azette appreciated the fact that Andrew was trying to make the journey as interesting as possible for her, and she was determined not be a wet blanket. Her spirits rose when they crossed a vast stretch of heather and gorse; the splendour of the red flushed sky astounded her. The sun was seemingly going down on her sorrow; she would be in another county when it rose, perhaps she would have another chance to find happiness. Andrew adjusted his sun visor, and told her stories of the Moor until they reached Princetown where they stopped to watch the graceful movements of some wild ponies.

When they drove on, Boy awoke from his comfortable position on the back seat, and thrust his silky head over Azette's shoulder. Presently she nodded off and had a strange dream. She was standing in the hallway of the Gordon's farmhouse, suddenly a woman stepped out of the shadows; her face was indistinct. Despite that, Azette knew she was Andrew's wife.

18

It was dark when they reached the Gordon's farmhouse, but the moon shone on its slate roof, and a light streamed from the open front door. Azette felt at home directly she set foot in the hall; Mrs Gordon greeted her kindly. She was a fine looking woman with alert blue eyes, and a cheerful manner. She asked:

'I hope the long drive has not tired you dear?'

'I do feel rather sleepy,' Azette confessed. 'One moment we were on Dartmoor, and it seemed the next moment Andrew was pointing out Cornish buildings.' She laughed at herself.

'That time lapse can be accounted for because Azette was asleep when we crossed the Tamer, Mother,' Andrew laughed teasingly. He was in a very good humour, and glad to be home.

Azette found herself glancing round the cream washed hallway in case his wife should step out of the shadows; but there was only Andrew's father waiting to greet her. When Azette looked up at his strong rugged face, and met his friendly brown eyes, she knew instinctively she was going to like him.

'I have been looking forward to meeting you, Azette. I must show you over the farm, and, in exchange you must tell me how you farm in the Channel Isles.' He clapped his hand on Andrew's shoulder. 'And now for a drink, and a bit to eat eh?'

A cold supper was laid on a gate-legged table in the dining-room; the windows were flung open and moths had stolen in from the night, and were hovering round the central light. Andrew and Azette had stopped for an evening meal on the journey down, but it was such a hot night that merely to bite into a piece of cold crisp lettuce would be a pleasure. Azette was seated

between Mr and Mrs Gordon, whi
Andrew was seated on his mothei s
right. A place had been set between him
and his father. Was it for Andrew's wife?
But he did not appear to expect
anybody. Mr Gordon carved a piece of
gammon, then filled four tankards with
cider. Who was the fifth one for? Boy
came in from the kitchen where he had
been at a water bowl; he pricked up his
ears when a car drew up outside the
farmhouse. It was late for visitors;
Azette was uneasy when she heard
footsteps in the hall.

A young man strode in and kissed
Mrs Gordon on her cheek; Azette
would have known him for her son
anywhere.

'Cheers,' cried Andrew. 'Nice to see
you again Ian. Couldn't Barbara make
it?'

'She's not going out in the evenings
whilst Craig is teething, it's too much
to expect from a baby sitter. But you
are all to spend tomorrow evening with
us.'

Ian offered his hand to Azette when his brother introduced him. Although two years older than Andrew, he appeared that much younger; this was doubtless due to his light hearted air. His blue eyes sparkled merrily when Mr Gordon filled the fifth tankard, and handed it to him.

'To you Azette,' he toasted her before taking his place next to his brother.

As the meal proceeded, there was laughter and family chaffing into which Azette was swiftly drawn; she could almost be in her Jersey farmhouse again.

★　★　★

When Azette opened her eyes the next morning, she looked straight into those of a young Scot, they were brown brooding eyes set in a strong rugged face. His portrait could have been painted a hundred years ago. He was surely an ancestor of Andrew's. Her eyes travelled past the open curtains, and an oak dressing table, to a linen press near the door. A pretty little girl, wearing a peacock-green frock, was perched on top of the press watching her.

'Can I talk to you now?' Her voice was crystal clear.

'That would be nice,' Azette smiled.

The child slid off the press and, when she crossed to the window, Azette saw that her hair was not quite red and not quite brown.

She explained, 'Granny said I wasn't to talk until you woke up.'

'I hope you did not have to wait too long. You must be Christabel.'

Christabel was peering out of the window. 'Uncle Andrew said I mustn't bring my little friend to show you. I had to leave him in the yard.'

'Never mind, I'll meet him later. Is that the chicken run over there?' Azette pointed to a large pasture enclosed by wire netting.

'Yes. Uncle Andrew is helping Grandad pack some eggs.' Christabel looked hard at a pink tin standing on the dressing table.

'Would you like some of that talcum powder Christabel?'

'Yes please.' Azette smiled as the child sprinkled powder inside the front of her frock. 'What is this powder called Zette?'

'Remember.'

'That's a funny name.'

It was silly name too, thought Azette, for somebody to use who wanted to forget. She could hardly believe Dennis was to marry Mandy today. She cheered somewhat when she was drinking tea in the kitchen with Mrs Gordon. Andrew's mother was a naturally cheery person; she also appeared to be the sort of woman who would not shy when faced with any task, but who would go forward determinedly to meet it.

'We like to have a break when Andrew comes down,' she said. 'This afternoon we will drive to the beach with Barbara and the children for a picnic tea; that means preparing an early lunch.' She set her empty cup down firmly, and turned to the vegetable rack.

Azette was beside her quickly. 'I'll prepare the vegetables, Mrs Gordon.'

'Thank you, that will give me a chance to get on with the breakfast Azette. Andrew told me you liked swimming?'

Azette could say she did without blushing. She and Andrew had been stark when swimming together, but it had seemed a natural state, and Andrew had not attempted to lay a hand on her. She was sure his mother would have understood if she had known how it had been. Azette would have asked her if Andrew was married, but feared this might sound as if she had designs on him — which she had not of course. When she stepped into the yard to throw vegetable peelings in the pig bin, Christabel was waiting for her.

'You haven't met my little friend yet, Zette.'

'Azette,' corrected Mr Gordon entering the yard. 'Did you sleep well, Azette?'

'Very well thank you Mr Gordon.'

'Then you'll be ready to walk round the farm with us after breakfast,' he observed as Andrew joined them.

Azette sensed this was going to be a happy day, and looked questioningly at Andrew as if seeking his confirmation. He gave her a reassuring grin, then Christabel stepped forward with cupped hands.

'Here is my little friend,' she announced gravely. She carefully exposed an enormous spider. 'His name is Claude.'

Claude was housed in a bucket, then Andrew swung Christabel up on his shoulders, and carried her down a lane to where his brother was waiting to take her home. Mr Gordon was eager to hear further details of the farms belonging to Azette's parents, and refused to let the conversation stray into other channels during their breakfast. A Mrs Trelawney arrived from the village in time to washup; whilst Andrew and Azette stacked crockery on the draining board, she gave them curious looks which could mean anything. Afterwards when Andrew caught hold of Azette's hand as they crossed the yard to the egg packing shed, she guessed the woman was staring after them from the kitchen window. Doubtless, when she returned to her cottage, she would either tell her husband that Andrew had been 'caught' by a girl at last, or tell him it was 'shocking' how some married men carried on — this according to Andrew's state.

Azette spent an interesting morning with Andrew and his father; they inspected the poultry runs, the Dutch barn, the up-to-date pig styes, the turnip field, the clover field and a pasture where a herd of Fresians grazed. Amongst them were five or six Jerseys; Azette watched intently as they cropped at the lush grass. Then Ian (who was responsible for the dairy herd) appeared and they followed him

271

to a cow-shed to admire a new born Fresian calf.

'What has Christabel called her Ian?' his father asked suspiciously.

'Er — Black Lace,' Ian responded rather uncomfortably. 'The name of Barbara's talcum powder I'm afraid.'

Mr Gordon bristled. 'That's what comes of letting women choose names. You can't beat Dolly, Daisy or Molly for a cow.'

'I agree,' said Andrew. 'But it becomes complicated when you have a herd of sixty doesn't it Dad?'

Mr Gordon noted how Azette's eyes blazed with pleasure when she leaned over the stall to view a dainty calf whose hide was the colour of *cafe-au-lait*. He tapped Ian's arm.

'How about asking Azette to name this Jersey calf if she will?'

Azette took this suggestion seriously. 'My mother has always owned a Jersey called 'Coffee', Mr Gordon.'

''Coffee', it shall be then Azette,' Mr Gordon agreed with surprising meekness.

Azette noted that Ian was winking at Andrew, they must share a private joke. The four of them turned back towards the pastures and discussed the merits of Fresians and Jerseys until Mr Gordon consulted his watch.

'Oh my, twelve o'clock already, and we're to have an early lunch today.'

'Twelve o'clock,' Azette echoed to herself. Dennis had been due to marry Mandy at eleven forty-five. Azette felt a traitor because she had not been aware of the time then, but she could not decide whom she had betrayed.

★　★　★

Afterwards Azette thought of that day as being a halcyon day. Immediately after lunch Ian deposited his wife, children and beach gear at the front gate; he could not join the party until later. Mrs Gordon left Mrs Trelawney to clear away the lunch things, her husband was driving their estate car out of the garage; it *had* to accommodate everybody and everything; under Mrs Gordon's breezy directions it did. The beach was sandy the sea was warm and baby Craig forgot his teething troubles and was soon splashing happily in a pool with his sister. Mr Gordon went for a walk across the sands with Andrew and Boy. Mrs Gordon vowed she would be first in the sea, she, like Azette and Barbara, wore a swimming costume under her frock; the girls laughingly tried, but failed, to beat her to it.

Barbara was a merry girl with neat features, blue eyes and short brown hair; she was easy going, but one word of reprimand was sufficient to bring her daughter to heel.

'Enjoying yourself Azette?' Andrew asked later as he swam alongside her.

'Yes, yes,' she answered emphatically.

This appeared to satisfy him for he left her to help Barbara with the children. He built a sand castle for Christabel with three towers, two small girls came up and planted toy windmills in two of the towers. When they spun slowly in the lazy wind; Christabel asked why her mother had not brought her toy windmill down.

'You are old enough to decide what you need on the beach Christabel,' Barbara said as she wiped sand off Craig's mouth.

Andrew decorated the third tower with a shell, then sat on the sands beside Azette who was drying her hair. She liked to have him beside her. Soon they looked round and laughed as Ian called from the roadway. He slammed, and locked, his car door, jumped down on the sands and hurried towards his family whilst shedding his clothes and shoes carelessly as he walked. By the time he reached Barbara's side he had stripped to his swimming trunks; without a word he pulled her to her feet and raced her down to the sea.

'You never did succeed in teaching that boy to be tidy,' Mr Gordon remarked to his wife with a laugh.

★ ★ ★

The evening, spent at Ian's home, passed as pleasantly as the afternoon; Azette relaxed on a settee beside Andrew whilst Barbara and Ian gaily handed round drinks and sandwiches. Barbara had changed into a pink frock and looked very pretty, Mrs Gordon was charming in a smart navy and white frock, Azette wore a white frock threaded with gold; Andrew told her she looked enchanting. Later in the evening they watched a thriller on the television; they were unaware that night had fallen until Ian switched on the light at the end of the play. Mr Gordon opened all the car's windows before driving his wife, Azette and Andrew home. Scents of the night came to them, but the air was oppressive, and they could see the Fresians moving restlessly in the pastures.

Mrs Gordon and Azette shared a pot of tea in the sitting-room whilst Mr Gordon put the car away, and Andrew let Boy out for a run. When Azette sought him out to say good night, she found him in the yard.

'Thank you for a perfect day, Andrew.' She reached up and kissed his warm cheek.

'It was a pleasure, Azette.' He too kissed her cheek. 'Now, it's up to you to set the pace.'

'Why?'

'If you don't, how shall I know when you feel free to love again?'

★ ★ ★

The next morning when Azette joined Mrs Gordon in the kitchen, she said there would be a storm before the day was out. She could tell by the humidity and falling barometer. Christabel tapped on the outer door; she looked most angelic as she handed her grandmother a bunch of wild flowers.

'Here are your Sunday flowers Granny.' She offered her face to be kissed. 'My windmill is in that box in Azette's bedroom. Can I have it Granny please?'

Mrs Gordon repressed a sigh. 'Would you mind helping Christabel find her windmill, Azette? It's somewhere in the linen press which I'm afraid is very topsy-turvy.' She reached for the frying pan. 'I haven't put the bacon on yet.'

The contents of the linen press were certainly topsy-turvy; Azette was obliged to empty everything on to the floor before she found the toy windmill at the bottom.

'I must find some wind now,' Christabel squealed excitedly before she raced downstairs leaving Azette to return everything to the press.

She picked up books, crayons, knitting needles and cuddly toys before reaching for a handful of photographs which had fallen out of an album. As she replaced them between unused leaves she could not help noticing they were wedding photographs. The bride was dark and petite, and dressed in white. The groom was Andrew.

Why had he avoided telling her he was married? It was too soon after she had lost Dennis for her not to feel let down again. Last evening Andrew had said it was up to her to set the pace. Well, she would ensure that 'the pace' never left the ground.

19

'Your family are great Andrew,' Azette said as they drove away from his father's farm that afternoon.

'Thank you. They liked you too Azette, they meant it when they said they looked forward to seeing you again.'

Azette thought it could become too complicated if she stayed with Andrew's parents again; it would not be difficult for her to fall in love with him in her eagerness to forget Dennis. How strange his family had not mentioned his wife — perhaps she had run out on him — perhaps there was a child — perhaps she would never know the truth.

'There's going to be one hell of a storm,' Andrew predicted when he turned on to the Plymouth road.

'Aren't we crossing Dartmoor again?'

Azette was studying a map.

'Not this trip; look at that black sky ahead.'

The whole countryside was waiting for something to happen; but nature kept it in suspense, trees were hushed and afraid to move a leaf for fear it would prevent them hearing warning signals. How different it would be had Dennis been at the wheel. The prospect of an adventurous drive over the Moor would lure him on, then, because they were together, something would have gone very wrong. Where was Dennis now? Where had he and Mandy spent the night? But Azette did not want to think of them together, she was disturbed by the haunting memory of Dennis. His easy laughter came to her through the open window, and his quick movements were to be seen in the antics of boys chasing each other round a field. Presently Azette folded the map and leant back, it was easy to relax when with Andrew.

It started to rain cautiously as though

the storm cloud overhead was feeling its way; it stood out against the yellow sky, and appeared to be outlined in brass. Andrew slowed down when a group of children ran out from a lane. He drew level with them when the storm-cloud burst; they were dumbfounded.

'Azette, ask them to shelter in here.'

She threw open the doors, and five grubby children crowded in the back of the car with Boy, whilst a lively boy scrambled on her knee. The rain beat loudly on the car roof and lashed at the windows; it was coming down in torrents, flooding the gutter and screening the fields. The car became an isolated unit.

'What's going to happen?' asked a scared voice from behind Andrew.

He turned round and gave a disarming grin. 'Nothing very terrible, old chap. We shall stay here until the rain stops, and you are all welcome to shelter with us.' He reached out and patted his dog's head. 'Boy likes children.' As if to prove his master's words, Boy started to lick the face of a small girl. 'No Boy. This little girl is *not* an ice lolly.'

The little girl giggled, Azette laughed loudly and the children lost their growing fears. Names were exchanged and, at Andrew's suggestion, one of the boys started to sing, soon everybody joined in. They progressed from song to song, jostling and treading on each other's toes, whilst Andrew handled the situation with infinite patience.

'It's stopped raining,' a child cried.

'Good,' said Andrew. 'I'll see you across the road, then you must all run straight home.'

Andrew crossed the children who turned to wave good-bye to Azette; she waved back. How absurd it was, when the car had been packed with grubby children she had learnt the depth of her feelings for Andrew. She must be wary. Her love for him could never compare with the love she had for Dennis. That love must have been with her from the time of her birth; she had accepted it as a natural thing, and had not realized how it was flourishing until too late. The love she was beginning to feel for Andrew was something entirely different. It could be exciting because of its newness, it could be passionate because Andrew had always had the power to rouse her emotions, it could be companionable because she shared Andrew's interest in farming, it could mean security because she had always been able to turn to him to talk over her troubles. But it must not mature because Andrew was married. Even though she could not understand why he had concealed this from her, she owed him a great deal, and this was a good time to thank him before they drove through the outskirts of Plymouth.

'I'll always remember how you did everything you could to help me when I was worried over Dennis and Mandy, Andrew,' she started. 'And this weekend you have been absolutely great. Thank you.'

'It hasn't been very difficult to help you Azette,' he responded blandly. 'Not difficult at all, because I've been falling in love with you all summer.'

'You mustn't do that,' she insisted sharply. 'I'll be leaving Tollbury very soon. I am to visit my aunts in turn. They are my father's sisters, Catherine and Anne; they often stay at the farm, it was their home until they married bank clerks who are now retired bank managers. Uncle Bernard lives on the outskirts of London, he could find me a job in the City.'

'You're not the type who could be happy working in London,' expressed Andrew forcefully.

'But it will be a complete change. It will give me a chance to explore London, and give me a chance to forget.'

'Very well, Azette, go to London and forget Dennis, and then come back to me. I'll be waiting for you. But let's get this straight Azette, I want you like parched earth wants water, but I'll

285

never share you with any man. I'll not share you either in body or in thought.'

Before Azette could answer Andrew's unexpected declaration, he had started the car, and they were part of a procession of cars heading for Plymouth. It astounded Azette that he, a married man, should have the impertinence to expect so much from her.

★ ★ ★

Immediately they entered the flat on their return to Tollbury, Azette sensed trouble. Jane's dejected stance, as she stood under the light glancing through a Sunday paper, told her that, given time, Jane would tell everything. She would make coffee, and she was sure Andrew was hungry.

'I spent the afternoon with the family,' Jane announced when the three of them gathered round the sitting-room table. 'That's why I'm togged up.' She stirred sugar into her coffee before springing her surprise. 'The family agree it would be a good idea if I flew to join Mum and Dad in South Africa. I told you Mum has been ill Azette.' Jane turned to Andrew and told him about the letter she had received from her father. 'I shall give my notice to Mr Bury tomorrow. When will you have finished typing Uncle George's book, Azette?'

'Within two weeks.'

'Why not take over from me as dental receptionist? The pay is good enough to enable you to keep on this flat.'

'No thanks, I don't want to stay on in Tollbury. How long will you be away Jane?'

'About a year.'

'Michael will miss you.'

'He won't. Michael has thrown me over.' Jane leaned back in her chair, rested her hands on the edge of the table and waited for Andrew's and Azette's reactions.

Andrew cut into the cheese, then shot Jane a look which plainly said he was surprised Michael had not thrown her over long ago.

Azette checked herself from saying that Jane had asked for it, and said softly, 'Do you want to talk about it Jane?'

'Yes, then you can both say, 'I told you so',' Jane cried crossly. She nibbled at a piece of cheese. 'Something terrible happened last evening. Mandy had left for good, Michael was to move to Poole today and was having a business talk with his father, so I felt pretty low. I went to the *Silver Anchor*; it was packed with holiday makers, and I didn't see anybody to talk to until Taffy and his crowd came in.'

Andrew raised his brows. 'Taffy is a drug addict isn't he?'

'Don't spit his name out like that, he's up at University and quite brilliant,' Jane flared up again. 'He asked me to a party.' She hurried on. 'It was in a bungalow in Green Lane. We drank and smoked, had coffee and crisps and I didn't think there was anything wrong until there was a thundering at the front door. There was a panic. Taffy pushed me out of a sash window, threw my shoulder bag out after me, slammed the window and drew the curtains. It was a police raid.'

'Did the police find you?' questioned Andrew harshly.

'No. It was easy to jump off the window sill into the yard. I was sneaking out of the back gate when who should pass but Michael. I was a fool to tell him what had happened.' Jane looked at Andrew and Azette in turn, her eyes pleaded and her pretty mouth trembled. 'Michael was furious. He said he had warned me all summer to keep clear of Taffy's crowd. He said he never wanted to see me again. Would you believe he could be so cruel?'

'Michael has never been cruel,' insisted Andrew. 'I've known him since the days when my brother and I spent holidays at Warren Farm.' He regarded Jane unfeelingly. 'By God, but you've had this coming to you for a long time Jane. That's a corny remark, but it's true,' he sighed. 'We must keep this from your family, they don't deserve it,' he finished tiredly.

★　★　★

Later that week Azette's mother wrote to say Dennis had turned up at his home in St Helier; he had received a warm welcome from his parents. They were delighted he had married that sweet girl Mandy. Because Mandy was Mandy, and so warm hearted and lovable, both his parents overlooked the fact that a baby was due shortly. They were proud of Dennis's success and were doing their utmost to find him a home in Jersey.

By the same post there was a letter addressed jointly to Jane and Azette from Mandy. She wrote that she was happy to be back home because her step-mother was kind and thoughtful. Mandy was, of course, looking forward to joining Dennis in Jersey after the birth of their child which the doctor said would be quite soon.

'Mandy is your cousin-in-law now,' Jane reminded Azette.

'That's so,' agreed Azette doing her best to sound pleased.

But of course she liked Mandy and, whenever she passed the closed door of her old flat, she pictured how the girl had sat by her sitting-room window in the evenings smocking children's frocks to make a nest egg for her child. Azette avoided Andrew as much as possible now, it would be foolish to risk a second unhappy love affair.

* * *

Once Jane had come to a decision she acted promptly; she handed in her notice to Mr Bury, booked a seat on a plane to South Africa and told her landlord of her plans. She packed some of her things which she planned to store at Warren House, and one evening Andrew agreed to call at the flat to collect two of her larger cases.

'If you want to shut these cases properly, you'll have to lighten the load, Jane,' he bellowed above the blare of her record player.

Azette thought Jane should have switched the player off as she knew Andrew hated the incessant beat of pop music. But Jane was in a difficult mood, alternatively pining for Michael, and cursing the police for dealing so harshly with her drug taking friends. Suddenly there came a loud pounding on the front door. Jane opened it, her face paled.

'It's the police,' she announced unnecessarily as a uniformed Inspector strode into the sitting-room and laid his hat on the table. He was followed by three plain clothes men and a pleasant policewoman; he gave Andrew (who was switching the record player off) a friendly nod, before taking down Azette's name and place of employment. Then he turned back to Jane.

'Have you had any visitors today who could have left Cannabis in your flat?'

'Er — ' Jane looked uncomfortable. 'Well, some friends were waiting in the hall for me when I came back from work. I asked them in for coffee.'

Whilst Jane gave the Inspector her friends' names, Azette watched two plain clothes men search the sitting-room. Suddenly she noticed a small round tin under the table, she had never seen it before, it could have rolled off the table. Supposing it contained Cannabis! She wondered how Jane felt, the flat was in her name. She frowned worriedly as a policeman picked up the small tin from under the table.

'What's in here?' he asked Jane.

'Snuff,' Jane replied in a strained voice.

During the hush whilst the man struggled to unscrew the lid, Azette glanced questioningly at Andrew. He gave her a reassuring wink. Then the awkward lid came off with a jerk, and fine brown snuff dusted the man's tweed jacket. He sneezed as he brushed it off.

'My uncle said he wanted to try snuff, so I bought that this afternoon,' Jane explained apologetically.

Nobody appeared to find that amusing. One of the men went to the bathroom, another to the kitchen (Azette heard the clink of crockery and clatter of saucepans) the third was in the bedroom and the fourth had now given his attention to Jane's suitcases; the policewoman helped him empty them. Jane was plainly wilting, but at last the Inspector told her:

'We'll be off now. Your flat is clean, but I'd watch what company you keep Miss Marley.'

Directly the police left, Jane burst into tears. 'This is the end,' she sobbed. 'I'd never have taken drugs in a thousand years. I never want to set eyes on Taffy's crowd again. I've been an awful fool; now I've lost Michael, and he's the only man I've ever loved.'

'Some day, some time, you'll be given a second chance Jane,' Andrew told her kindly.

Azette said nothing, but thought it was surprising how a show of tears could move a man.

'It is nice of you to say that Andrew.' Jane accepted his handkerchief to mop her tears. 'I've often been bitchy to you. I felt awful when those boys turned the sheep into your oat field. You see I had told The Lion he ought to camp in your wood when they wanted to avoid the police. But I meant in Faraway Woods, not in that little wood by your oat field.'

At this point Azette hurriedly closed herself up in the kitchenette; it was best for Andrew to deal with Jane alone.

20

'Fancy,' twittered Miss Marley from her end of the luncheon table. 'Mandy has a baby already. I've had a letter from her. She was only married to Dennis a few weeks ago!'

'Isn't that what they call a Package Baby?' grunted the Professor. 'I don't know what Father would have said, but then marriage is not the 'in' thing Jane told me.'

Lady Monica pursed her lips undecisively. Azette was ready to spring to Dennis's defence; as if he could guess her thoughts, Andrew said:

'Mandy is a charming girl.' Andrew deliberately looked across at Lady Monica. 'Dennis will make a name for himself in the art world; Mandy and their baby are lucky.'

Lady Monica took her cue from Andrew. 'At least Dennis has done the right thing,' she chortled.

'Is it a boy or girl?' asked Michael who had only accepted an invitation to lunch because Jane had already flown to Africa.

'It's a little girl,' Miss Marley cooed. 'I must crochet a pink jacket.'

'I shall buy a pink blanket,' purred Lady Monica.

Miss Marley cut into the plum pie Curtis had set before her; when the juice flowed she chirruped, 'How clever of Mrs Curtis. It's pink.'

The Professor looked down the length of the table witheringly, then he gave his attention to Michael. 'I hope you have not given up sailing?'

'No Professor, I've moved my yacht to Poole Harbour. And I've taken up photography again more seriously. I'll take a coloured photograph of you all after lunch.'

Azette was relieved to see Michael looking so cheerful; she formed the impression that he realized his break with Jane was all for the best.

'You must visit us whenever your business brings you this way Michael,' the Professor told him. 'I'll be deuced quiet here without you young people. Jane gone, Andrew soon to move into his farmhouse and Azette off to London.'

'London is such a wicked place they say.' Miss Marley's eyes were troubled.

'Rubbish May,' the Professor growled. 'Azette is far too sensible to get into trouble any damn where. There will always be a welcome for you at Warren House Azette.'

Lady Monica added graciously, 'Yes, we shall be delighted if you could find time to stay with us before your return to Jersey Azette.'

There was a confident ring in Andrew's voice as he observed, 'I'm sure Azette does not intend to walk out of our lives for good.'

★ ★ ★

'Azette does not intend to walk out of our lives for good.' Azette recalled these

298

words of Andrew's when she was on the Waterloo train two days later. She did wish she had been able to say good-bye to Andrew. Yesterday he had not been in for lunch; he had driven to the hills to see Yaffle, but she had hoped to encounter him when she walked round Warren Farm in the early afternoon. It had become a part of her life; she had kept a tab on everything; yesterday a field had been made ready to receive autumn sowings of wheat, now the soil was open to the air and light. Today the maincrop was to be lifted by the potato spinner. Azette had said good-bye to Mr and Mrs Posser, and to Green and his young wife, but there had been no signs of Andrew. Work was still progressing on the rebuilding of his farmhouse. Unglazed windows had robbed the roofless house of expression, sawdust had clung to weeds in the garden and cement had been mixed where the bluebells had bloomed. In the orchard apples were ready to be picked.

Why had Andrew not been frank with her, and told her he was married? What was he doing now? Perhaps he was in the library where woodland creatures looked out of their cases with glassy eyes. They were all there, excepting the deer. She had never come across a deer, it was too late now.

And Dennis — did he think of her as he trod the familiar streets of St Helier searching for a home for Mandy and their baby? Azette had visited Mandy in the Maternity Home; she looked blissfully happy. She shared Dennis's artistic temperament, and she had given him a bonny dark haired daughter; but she could never wander down a leafy lane with him, or cross a sandy beach by his side, and say 'Do you remember, Dennis, how when we were kids we — ' Azette's eyes were sad when she thought of the tiny mite, who bore a striking resemblance to Dennis, but she reminded herself that she had enabled this little girl to have her rightful father. Even though there might be occasions

300

when her heart ached for Dennis, her conscience would be untroubled.

★ ★ ★

Azette was met at Waterloo by her Aunt Catherine's husband, Uncle Bernard. He insisted on carrying both her cases.

'I may be an O.A.P. Azette, and a grandfather four times over, but I've kept myself fit — golf, tennis and a daily turn round the common.' Azette kept close to Uncle Bernard, and followed him up an incline as a crowd surged round them with a roar. 'It's very quiet here this time of the day,' Uncle Bernard shouted.

'Oh. What's it like in the rush hour then?'

'Absolutely chaotic.'

They were soon comfortably settled in the Hayes train with only two other people in their compartment. Azette looked out of the window in horror, there were houses everywhere and hardly a green thing to be seen.

'Is it like this at Hayes, Uncle Bernard?'

'My goodness no. Hayes is in the Garden of Kent.' He glanced at his watch. 'Catherine will have tea waiting for us, afterwards there will be time for me to have a turn on the Common with the dog, I like to be back for the six o'clock news.'

Azette was so happy to see her Aunt Catherine again. She was an attractive woman with placid green eyes; her hair, which had once been as fair as Azette's, was a pretty silver.

Aunt Catherine's neat house was practically run by electricity. It peeled potatoes, washed up, polished floors, cleaned teeth, killed flies and cut the garden hedge. After an effortless week-end, Azette felt restive. She would have liked to take the cairn terrier for a run over the Common, but this was Uncle Bernard's privilege.

On Monday, armed with a map, and a letter of introduction to an Employment Agency from Uncle Bernard,

Azette braved London. She could not go wrong Aunt Catherine said, the line started at Hayes and terminated at Charing Cross. Azette tried not to act like a raw country girl; when the train crossed the glittering Thames her heart uplifted. But when she stepped out of Charing Cross Station into the crowded Strand, she felt as though she had been thrown to the lions.

The Employment Agency found Azette a post immediately. As she could not decide when she wished to return to Jersey, she had signed on as a relief typist; for five days a week she joined the rush hour crowds from Hayes to London, at the weekends she relaxed at Aunt Catherine's comfortable home.

She often thought of Tollbury; she wrote to the Professor and his sisters, and they wrote back. She did not write to Andrew, neither did he write to her; but Michael sent her a photograph she had taken of him wearing his deer-stalker. She fixed it in her mirror, and Aunt Catherine teased her. Azette kept the photograph of the family group in her writing case; she frequently studied it because Andrew was so disturbingly handsome. In November she had an airmail from Jane; it was not descriptive, she simply said she had settled down happily enough because she realized her presence was good for her mother. Azette heard nothing from Dennis, but Mandy sent a card to say they were staying in rooms in St Helier until they found something more suitable.

One Saturday morning Aunt Catherine and Uncle Bernard were to attend a banker's funeral. Azette offered to look after Bingo, the Cairn terrier; he was a game little dog, after breakfast she groomed him until his fawn coat shone. The Common was five minutes from the house, Azette liked to walk under silver birch and to pass clumps of heather and gorse. She went as far as Keston Windmill, then crossed the road, and made her way through golden bracken to the Ponds. She sat on a bench and contemplated the reflections in the water; children played nearby. Presently she noticed a dark haired man was sketching on the opposite bank. He could be Dennis; he wore a grey jersey and was of similar build. Dennis could have called on the London art gallery who acted as his agents, he could then have caught the Hayes train to visit Aunt Catherine who was his second cousin. On finding nobody in at her home, he could be passing the time sketching, and would call again later.

Azette put Bingo on his lead, calmly stepped over roots of trees, and circled the pond until there were only blackberry bushes between her and the artist. He sat on a tree stump sharpening his pencil. When he examined the point, his eyes met Azette's; how could she have mistaken him for Dennis?

Azette walked on, and stopped at Keston for a drink and a sandwich; then she wandered over farmland thinking back to the time when her relationship with Dennis had changed. They had been lost on the headland, Dennis had said he felt they were not meant to be more than friends. He had told her that her mother had once expected his father's child; knowing this had caused him to feel even closer to her than a cousin. This surprising news had made her wonder whether there was not something left over from their parents' romance which was making itself felt between them now. She had wrongly imagined it had been given to her and Dennis to take up that short lived love affair. She had foolishly ignored the fact that Dennis's kisses never aroused her as Andrew's did.

She had placed Dennis in an unenviable position by clinging to him too tenaciously when he learnt that Mandy was expecting his child. He had felt honour bound to marry Mandy with whom he must have been more than a little in love with even then. But he must have also felt honour bound to marry her because, since their child-hood, it had been a point of honour between Dennis and herself never to break promises made to each other.

The sun had come out. Azette had climbed a hill and was back on the Common. She let Bingo off his lead; he was glad to be free. She too felt free. When she had seen the artist was not Dennis, she had been glad. She had been glad because at that moment she admitted to herself she had never loved Dennis in the way a woman can love a man. Her love for him had been the love one can have for a close relative, but nothing stronger.

★   ★   ★

Late November was foggy, Azette longed for the milder climate of Jersey. She wanted to spend Christmas with her family, but was not ready to share celebrations with Dennis, Then a letter came from Mandy. They had been unable to find a suitable studio in

Jersey, but Dennis's old friend, Mark (whose own studio was to be pulled down to make room for a super-market) had bought property on the hillside above St Peter Port, and, as this Guernsey house was large enough for two artists and their families, Mark had asked Dennis to share it with him. They were to move to Guernsey in mid December. Azette could go home for Christmas after all, and there was still time to visit Aunt Anne.

Aunt Anne and Uncle Leslie had retired to a house on the edge of the New Forest. It closely resembled the house in Hayes, and Uncle Leslie resembled Uncle Bernard which was not surprising as Aunts Catherine and Anne had similar tastes. Aunt Anne also had a Cairn terrier; he was called Whoops, but Azette often called him Bingo, so he seldom obeyed her when she took him walking in the New Forest.

During these walks Azette thought less and less of Dennis and more and more of Andrew, although this could lead nowhere. One evening Michael telephoned her. Had she realized how close to him she was now? She had not, but, now that she did, she was eager to see him again. Aunt Anne invited Michael to Sunday dinner; afterwards Michael and Azette walked Whoops in the New Forest.

'I've been up to my eyes in work,' Michael told Azette in response to her enquiries as to how he was managing the Estate Office at Poole. 'But I have a smashing secretary.'

'Blonde or brunette?'

'Er — sort of medium. It's her marvellous smile that gets me.'

'Perhaps she will crew for you next spring Michael.'

'Hold on, I've only just had the courage to ask her to a New Year's Ball,' Michael grinned. He told Azette more about his secretary as they walked through fallen leaves.

After Michael had paused to drag Whoops out of a rabbit's burrow, she asked urgently, 'Michael I must say good-bye to Andrew before I fly home to Jersey. How can I go about it?'

' 'Phone him at his farmhouse. He's living there now.'

'Alone?' she asked sharply.

'Yes, Andrew is quite alone.'

'I don't want to 'phone him, I'd rather see him personally.'

'Well then, the Marleys invited you to visit them, take up their offer. I could pick you up after I've closed the office next Saturday afternoon. I promised Mum I'd be home for the night. I'll drop you at Warren House first.'

21

When Azette and Michael looked down from the hillside on to Tollbury, the lights from the street lamps and houses made it appear larger than it was.

'I had another air-mail from Jane yesterday,' said Azette thinking of her then.

'How is she?'

'She says she was glad she flew out as her mother is already better; they'll be home for good in another year. Don't you miss Jane, Michael?'

'Sometimes, but she led me a hell of a dance, and now there's Helen. At heart Jane was a kind person, she liked to be friendly with everybody, but wasn't discerning. Taffy's crowd wouldn't have let Jane go without a struggle, that's why it was best for her to leave Tollbury.'

Michael slowed down at the cross-roads outside Tollhouse Café; Azette wondered how the tatty parrot was. It seemed more than seven months since she and Dennis had chased the bird across the heath. She hoped Dennis had settled down happily in Guernsey; now he was able to realize his ambition to paint Mandy's portrait.

The Marleys were delighted to see Azette; Michael had been right when he had said that childless people often felt cut off from life. In winter Warren House seemed especially isolated; the occupants retired early, and soon after ten Azette was tucked up in bed with a stone hot water bottle at her feet. She was in the room that had once been Jane's, some of her frocks still hung in the wardrobe; they had a forlorn air. Azette fell asleep thinking of Jane, and of the good natured way in which she had let her share her flat. She awoke thinking of Andrew.

'Would you like your curtains opened Miss Renouf?' Curtis inquired on entering with Azette's early tea.

'Yes please Curtis.'

The sky was gloomy. Curtis lit the old fashioned gas fire before he left the bedroom soundlessly; when the room had warmed up, Azette slid out of bed and went to the window. It faced south and she could see the headland where the jungle thrived. Beyond it was the wreck of the *Emma*; fishermen had said they could hear the young wife cry out for her children. Andrew's wife might have run away with another man. She could be living in the West Country, she could turn up at Warren Farm at any time. Azette wondered whether she had been foolish to have sought Andrew out merely to say good-bye. Undoubtedly she had been foolish not to question him about his marriage before she left Tollbury.

Later that morning the Professor drove Azette and his sisters to Church; he hated driving, and only took his Ford out when it was absolutely essential. Azette sat beside him and listened sympathetically to his explosive comments when cars came towards them at over 30 miles an hour. The drivers were cretins, those who overtook him were road hogs, and those who drove away from the Church were blasted heathens. Miss Marley said nothing, her thoughts were far away; Lady Monica assumed the demeanour of Lady Bountiful, and bowed graciously to villagers as they neared the Church. They sat in the family pew where Marleys had sat for generations.

'It was a beautiful service,' twittered Miss Marley on their return home. She adjusted the cushion of her Sheraton chair before Curtis handed coffee to her, Lady Monica and Azette. (The Professor was calming down in his study aided by a brew of Jasmine tea.) 'Now I must ask Mrs Curtis what she can spare for my bird table.' Miss Marley set down her coffee cup, and left her sister to entertain Azette.

'You look very smart in that cream wool frock Azette,' Lady Monica declared approvingly.

'Thank you; I bought it in the West End. Lady Monica, would you mind if I went for a walk this afternoon? I — I would like to call on Andrew.'

'That's a charming idea Azette, I fear Andrew has become rather a lonely person.' Lady Monica had been petting her white poodles, now she left them to their own devices as a more important matter claimed her attention. 'Once I had hoped that Jane and Andrew would marry, but it was not to be.'

'But Lady Monica,' Azette could not help pointing out. 'Andrew isn't free to marry.'

'Not free! Good gracious, what makes you say that?'

'I thought he was married.'

'He was, but surely you know what happened to his wife Mary.'

'No. Andrew has never mentioned her to me. Are they divorced?'

'My dear girl — . But I see you know nothing of his sad story.' Lady Monica studied Azette with increasing interest. 'I do not wish to be impertinent,

Azette, but what are your feelings for Andrew?'

'He is so understanding, we have much in common and I could love him very much.'

'In that case it would be unfair of me not to tell you what happened soon after he was married. One day his wife drove to her parents' home to collect some of her belongings, she drove along a motorway; there was a pile-up and she was killed instantly.'

'Oh no!' Azette paled. 'How terrible. What a frightful time it must have been for Andrew.'

'It certainly was. Old Mr Gordon had recently died, and had left Warren Farm to Andrew. It was a fine old house, probate had been granted and Andrew was due to move into the farmhouse with Mary after having necessary decorations carried out for her.' Lady Monica sighed. 'You can imagine what an ordeal it was for Andrew when he had to move into Warren Farm alone.'

So this was the 'terrible happening'

which Mrs Yaffle had spoken of. 'Oh, but why didn't Andrew tell me about Mary?' Azette cried distressfully.

'He was so shocked that he could not bear to talk about her. We have known Andrew since he was a schoolboy, he and his brother would spend holidays with their great uncle. We became very fond of those boys, and did what we could to cheer Andrew. He was desperately unhappy and asked us not to mention his loss to anybody, so, with the exception of Mrs Yaffle, everybody in the district thought he was unmarried.'

'Didn't Jane know the truth?'

'No because she was in Africa at that time. When she came to Tollbury she was so bright and gay that I thought she might make a suitable wife for Andrew.'

'I understand everything now,' said Azette slowly. Andrew was naturally reserved when it came to talking about his private life; Azette could forgive him for not feeling equal to discussing such a tragedy with her. He could have been in no hurry to have his farmhouse rebuilt because he had planned to bring his bride to the original building, and, after he had lost her, he must have often imagined she was there with him in spirit. When the farmhouse was destroyed by fire, he could have felt her death even more keenly. Azette's eyes were misty when she turned to Lady Monica. 'So that's why Andrew's family avoided mentioning his wife. Thank you for telling me everything Lady Monica, and thank you for helping Andrew.'

'Perhaps it has been given to you to comfort Andrew,' Lady Monica suggested hopefully.

They heard the gong, and rose to their feet.

★ ★ ★

That afternoon Azette stood at the gate of Warren Farmhouse. It was roofed with burnt clay tiles, smoke rose from a chimney, but the uncurtained windows gave it an unlived in air. The front garden was clear of weeds, a robin was perched on a fork dug into the newly turned soil. The sky was grey, a damp chill prevailed; Azette wore a classic camel coat and high brown boots, she had bought them in the West End in an overheated store; they had seemed too warm then. She opened the gate and walked unhesitatingly down the path to the front door. There was, as yet, neither knocker or bell; she peered through the sitting-room window, it ran the length of the house and was furnished with only a piano and a stool. The dining-room was empty, one of its doors opened into the kitchen which contained a table, two chairs and kitchen equipment. Its outer door led into a small porch in which stood a pair of muddy gum boots. Azette's heart raced.

As she turned to the back of the house she noticed the trees in the orchard had lost their leaves, their branches were ungainly, she supposed Andrew would prune them soon. She skirted a stack of logs; it was not yet twilight but the table lamp in the study (which overlooked the back garden) was already lit. It made her feel shut out of the house. Andrew was writing at his desk; how handsome he looked with his copper hair, and bold, weather beaten, features. He wore a rust brown jersey, the one Azette had seen his mother knitting. Boy was stretched out on a rug in front of a wood fire, he moved uneasily, sprang up and barked until Andrew threw down his pen and spoke to him. Suddenly Andrew looked straight at Azette, then he was out of the study door in a flash. As he strode over the rough grass to her, she shivered uncontrollably; she knew for a certainty that she loved him.

'I — I.' She had forgotten how she had planned to greet him.

'Never mind your opening speech Azette; I knew you had to come back to me sometime, even so it's hard to believe you are here.' He reached out and touched her arm tentatively. 'You look cold, come in by the fire. Didn't you know it had started to rain?'

'No.'

'But there's rain on your face, it can't be tears, I've never seen you cry.'

She stepped from the garden into the hall. 'I'm staying at Warren House Andrew. I'm to fly home for Christmas from Exeter. I had to see you once again.'

'Why only once again?' he asked as they entered the study where a tape was playing Beethoven's Triple Concerto. 'I could stand up to seeing you every day.'

She smiled as she held her cold hands out to the fire, and watched the movements of the flames as they attacked a log.

'Would you like to take your coat off before you sit down?'

'Please, it's nice and snug in here.'

Andrew took refuge in commonplace remarks, he saw now that Azette's cheeks had been wet from tears, not from rain. He wanted to help her regain her poise.

'The builder advised me to turn on the heating everywhere to dry out the house. I'll show you round later. It's very under furnished at present.' He was helping her off with her coat. 'I aim to find pieces suited to a farmhouse, up to now I've played safe and bought only what I've needed.' He hung her coat over his desk chair whilst she seated herself on a settle. 'Tea or coffee?'

'Tea please, Andrew.'

As Boy followed Andrew out of the room, Azette thought of the time when she had sat beside him on Mrs Yaffle's settle and watched the bees in the Kilner jar go up and down.

'We could do with a small table here,' observed Andrew when he returned with a tea tray.

Azette removed some books from a stool. 'This will do for now.' She transferred the books to the far end of the settle. The easiest thing for her to say after that was, 'How are your sheep Andrew?'

'Fine. They came down from the hills

to clear the turnip tops; we clamped the turnips for the winter cattle feeding.' Andrew passed Azette her tea before sitting opposite her in a worn leather armchair, which she recognized as being one that had stood in the library at Warren House. 'Well, how did you like working in London Azette?'

'I missed the open country, but the three relief jobs I had were interesting, and I was able to look around London.' She described her experiences. 'One day I became hopelessly lost, there was nobody around to ask, then I wanted you Andrew. I've gone on wanting you ever since.' Her voice trailed off, but she found it again to admit, 'I made a mistake Andrew. Whilst I was away from Tollbury I learnt a lot about myself, I learnt that I had never loved Dennis in the way a woman loves a man. Because he shared my past I was afraid to face the future without him, but the past has gone and the future can hold a new happiness.'

'It will, Azette, if you marry me. I

promise you.' Andrew regarded her sympathetically. 'Believe me, I knew you were going through hell after Mandy had named Dennis as the baby's father; I tried to help you, then reasoned you were the only one who could deal with such a problem, and after you had, I realized you'd need time to recover.'

'Yes, it's true that time is a healer.' She looked at him sadly. 'Andrew, I only learnt this morning how you lost your wife.'

He replied gruffly, 'I should have told you about Mary myself, but it was a long time before I could accept her death. When I did, I couldn't bring myself to discuss her with anybody, I feared some people would be over sympathetic and make things worse.'

'You could have spoken of Mary to me Andrew,' Azette told him softly.

'I realize that now, but you had your own problems.' It was then that Andrew found relief in speaking of his wife until hailstones struck sharply on the panes.

Boy growled, Andrew rose to his feet and took up the tea tray.

'Who cooks for you?' Azette asked following him into the kitchen.

'Mrs Green and Mrs Posser work that out between them, and keep the dust down, though there's not much furniture to dust.'

'Show me round.'

'When I've kissed you.' He drew her into his arms and kissed her tenderly. 'I love you very, very much darling.'

'As I love you Andrew.' She twined her arms round his neck.

'You are going to marry me?'

'Of course I am.'

'I've wanted to make love to you ever since I first saw you in the café scullery, but I soon realized there was more to you than just sex. When you said you were going to marry Dennis, I cursed myself for being so slow.'

Soon they went from room to room unhurriedly, getting to know the feel of the house together. The rain stopped, from the sitting-room window they could see Dave and Sally Posser hurrying homewards in the wake of their parents. Dave wore a blue balaclava, and Sally wore a red knitted bonnet over her brown bunches.

'That's what I want for us,' mused Azette.

'Why not?' asked Andrew taking her hand. 'Life is going to begin again for us both.'

They watched a young deer running past the gate through the dusk. After it had vanished into a thicket, there were a thousand things to discuss — the best month for their wedding, the day on which Andrew could fly to Jersey for Christmas, the white goats they would keep in the orchard, the curtains Azette would make for Andrew, the carpets he would buy for her and the love they felt for each other.

We do hope that you have enjoyed reading this large print book.

Did you know that all of our titles are available for purchase?

We publish a wide range of high quality large print books including:
Romances, Mysteries, Classics
General Fiction
Non Fiction and Westerns

Special interest titles available in large print are:
The Little Oxford Dictionary
Music Book, Song Book
Hymn Book, Service Book

Also available from us courtesy of Oxford University Press:
Young Readers' Dictionary
(large print edition)
Young Readers' Thesaurus
(large print edition)

For further information or a free brochure, please contact us at:
Ulverscroft Large Print Books Ltd.,
The Green, Bradgate Road, Anstey,
Leicester, LE7 7FU, England.
Tel: (00 44) **0116 236 4325**
Fax: (00 44) **0116 234 0205**

Other titles in the
Linford Romance Library:

SEASONS OF CHANGE

Margaret McDonagh

When Kathleen Fitzgerald left Ireland twenty years ago, she never planned to return. In England she married firefighter Daniel Jackson and settled down to raise their family. However, when Dan is injured in the line of duty, events have a ripple effect, bringing challenges and new directions to the lives of Dan, Kathleen and their children, as well as Kathleen's parents and her brother, Stephen. How will the members of this extended family cope with their season of change?